The Casebook of
The Manleigh Halt
Irregulars

Edited by Philip Craggs

"Okay, I'll be off then. Got a sackful of tales and a head full of memories, off to dance under some other stars for a while. It's been fun. Love you all. Nothing to fear."

Matt Kimpton, 1976 - 2012

Obverse Books
Cover Design by Cody Quijano-Schell
First published December 2012

Obverse Books would like to thank
Gwenda, Donald, Rachel and Annie Craggs; Molly and Ray Doyley;
Baiba Auria; Michelle Hebborn; Eva and Istvan Szavai; Jim Smith;
Steve, Liz, Chris and Katie Mellish; Lucy Finnie and Jen Croydon; Tim
Maytom; Nick Wallace; Steve Cole; George Mann; Diana and Steve
Kimpton and Tom Winch; and, of course, Paul Magrs, Cody
Quijano-Schell and Stuart Douglas.

Printed and bound in Great Britain by inkylittlefingers

CONTENTS

The Last Waltz

Kati Szavai

The snow begins again, falling even heavier, dancing a dreary grey waltz outside. The American author decides to take a break. She clicks open her Schiaparelli handbag and pulls out a cigarette case. Checking her maroon lips in the shiny lid she pops the case open and takes out a Camel and a cigarette holder, picks up her Zippo and gazes into the flame rising from the single click of the lighter. She holds the Camel up into the light and puffs on it until the paper turns bright orange all around and the cigarette catches. The beauty of it often makes her forget where she is – not as much the place (that never mattered much anyhow), but the time, the sense of historical events fading into one another, headline following headline.

Engrossed, she fails to notice the old woman edging her way towards her. She would be easy to spot – the crowd of adoring young women gathering for Queenie's book signing look very much alike. The strong make-ups, the heavy woollen coats way out of style, the stink of those horrid perfumes that make Queenie feel truly sick - as though she were clean and immortal but all the time spreading an awful disease to those who can't afford to be fashionable and still try anyhow. They're called the Brits. Damn sailors. She takes a drag and checks her face again, worried that the radiant young look might go one day. The smoke dissolves in the reflection and Queenie gasps as a wrinkled face appears on the mirror of the silver lid, and a pair of bony hands reach towards her. Queenie's horror further increases as she recognises Clarissa Miller, *the* Clarissa Miller, from that night of fire and destruction, years older, and absolutely impossible. Clarissa, realising that Queenie has noticed her, reaches for Queenie's neck and Queenie, not wasting any time, dives off her chair under the table as the Schiaparelli handbag, the Camel and the Zippo fly in three different directions.

Dogberry had his 'unpleasant task' face on. Clarissa and Wilson hung their head and tried to look busy while Sergeant Whitney, largely unable to recognise finer facial expressions, greeted Dogberry with a cheery nod.

'Caught anything on the radio bulletin then? '

'Not much.' Dogberry sighed. 'What really worries me is the background chatter. It is completely gone.'

'Well, there's nothing much to listen to at the moment is there? Half an hour's news a day, maybe we're hearing the silence between programmes for the next few years?' suggested Whitney. 'I mean...' The previous evening Dogberry had explained to Whitney why exactly their radio had picked up transmissions from various weather forecasts from the station's very near future in the background of a news bulletin from their last stop in the 1940s. It took three hours, several charts, a lot of timelines and some aspirin. 'I mean,' Whitney added hastily, 'this is rather worrying.'

'It has its ups and downs, of course — quieter days and louder ones. It can even stop for a second or two — I expect this would be the effect of shifting in time. But it's never gone away entirely.' He glanced at Wilson and Clarissa, who had remained absolutely still up until this point, then announced: 'Clarissa.'

Clarissa and Wilson both sighed. Wilson returned to his newspaper, relieved, while Clarissa followed Dogberry to his desk.

'The American is doing a reading tonight.' Dogberry waved a poster at Clarissa. 'The radio lines have been weakening since she arrived in town.'

'I'm not surprised. That Queenie blurs any channel of information with her sheer stupidity.' Queenie was hailed as a feminist and Clarissa bought one of her novels years ago. It turned out to be a cheap romance. 'She's a flapper riding the moment, selling books to young girls who can't afford to live like her, going around in Chanel's newest design showing her legs and what women shouldn't aspire to...'

'You'll have to go and see more than her legs I'm afraid. You need to investigate,' said Dogberry, edging towards Wilson to have a glimpse of his paper.

'Why me?'

'Her fans are women. You'll blend in.' Wilson was working on a crossword puzzle which had completely distracted Dogberry from the conversation.

'I'll have to be Mae West to blend in with those girls...' Clarissa said with a shrug.

'Take her with you if you want,' Dogberry replied, no longer listening. 'No, no Wilson, four down can not possibly be 'ceramic', especially not spelt like that.'

Clarissa approached the bookshop like a wild animal sniffing around the zoo. She decided to wear her red summer jacket to seem edgier but seeing the crowd of young girls smoking by the entrance she realised everything she wore was out of fashion.

She made her way in and took a seat in the audience. Wilson would be less out of place in here than me, she thought. She herself had a reading in this shop once and although it didn't attract the same size crowd it still gave her some confidence that she knew the territory. As the fans all sat down the shop owner introduced Queenie. The girls started clapping as Queenie opened the staff door and walked to her chair, bowing and smiling and taking a few Charleston steps, trying to make her appearance in a small town bookstore's staff door as glamorous as possible.

Clarissa hardly recognised the femme fatale of the posters in this petite, smiling girl skipping to her chair in the cream colour knee-length dress showing her strong calves and healthy curves. Even the most dramatic make up couldn't disguise that she had a simple, pretty face – Clarissa almost liked her for a moment. Scanning the room, she spotted the three well-known young men, 'The Sheiks', who accompanied Queenie on her travels. The Sheiks were chatting to each other, smoking and obviously discussing the girls in the room. One of them reached into his jacket and pulled out a metal tin. He shook the tin with a wide grin and mouthed the word 'cocaine' to his mates. Clarissa's gaze left the boys and returned to Queenie, who has finished talking about her latest novel and the heroine's complex, but fun-loving character and turned to the audience to answer any questions. Dozens of hands rose to the air, and Clarissa lost sight of Queenie for a while.

I'd better go for a walk, she thought, before I say something I'll regret. The girls sighed and shuffled their seats back as she made her way to the aisle between the chairs. Clarissa was two chairs away from freedom when music started. Queenie jumped up to demonstrate the new craze in America that would show men how women have a good time and performed a seamless black bottom, as though that would solve anything. The music stopped and Clarissa, stuck between two girls who got up to dance along, lost her temper and shouted into the momentary silence: 'Isn't this lifestyle a complete acceptance of the idea that women are non-productive and must stay out of public life? Women were asked to work during the war then sent home as the men came back. Isn't fighting for our independence more important right now than being pretty and attractive?' All the heads turned towards her. She hastily added 'Which you do very well, of course.'

Queenie smiled and pointed at Clarissa:

'There you have it, ladies. As long as there are women prepared to ask questions womankind will always have hope.' She posed for the photographer as she clapped her manicured hands.

But Clarissa didn't care because she saw it. Just for a second, the moment between her question and Queenie's answer. Beneath Queenie's pearl embroidered jacket an oversize pendant hung on a fine silver chain. It was amber-coloured with a curious glow to it and it had a crack running down the right hand side. This pendant, hidden under a jacket and not matching anything, out of date even for her grandmother, was the only odd thing that made Clarissa realise that Dogberry might have been right - apart from the fact that Dogberry was always right. Tense, she grabbed her copy of Queenie's novel and sat through the rest of the show impatiently tapping her feet on the floor, waiting to queue up for the signing.

Queenie decided to take a break. She clicked open her Chanel handbag and pulled out a cigarette case. Checking her rouge in the shiny lid she popped the case open and took out a Lucky and her cigarette holder. Sliding the cigarette into the holder she picked up her Ronson Banjo lighter and gazed into the flame that rose from the single click of the button.

When she looked up the woman with that annoying question stood in front of her table, a copy of her book in one hand and an awful red jacket in the other.

'Which one do you want me to sign,' Queenie joked.

'Sorry.' Clarissa held out the book.

Queenie leafed through it with genuine interest. Clarissa suppressed a grimace at the professional vanity.

'Well, I'm glad you liked it.' Queenie said. 'Who do I make it out to?'

'Clarissa Miller. A writer myself.'

'Really?' Queenie signed the book, leafed through it again then handed it back. She took a long look at Clarissa. 'What sort of stories do you write?' But before Clarissa could answer, Queenie stopped her: 'We should have a chat over a drink – I heard there's a jazz band in town, what do you say?'

The old bar was full of shiny surfaces that evening: freshly cleaned mirrors reflecting the dimmed lights, glasses, bottles, golden brass and reed instruments and shimmering red lips and nails. The Sheiks, who followed Queenie and Clarissa in gloomy silence, finally left them and disappeared in the deep belly of the bar. Queenie and Clarissa found a table by the entrance – it was a busy spot. People kept brushing against the table and tripping over their chairs. Neither Clarissa nor Queenie seemed to notice that at all: their eyes were fixed on each other.

'So, what did you say you wrote?' Queenie asked.

'Feminist fiction. The New Woman of the twentieth century.'

'Same as me, then?'

'Very similar,' Clarissa nodded trying not to smirk.

Queenie leant forward, touching Clarissa's hand: 'But I think we have more in common.' Her sandals were tapping out the rhythm of the song and she added: 'More than anyone is this bar would think.'

Clarissa looked around at the fashion exhibits sipping their cocktails. One of the Sheiks was talking to a girl in a sequinned dress. Touching her shoulder and leaning close to her ears he was shouting over the music. She pouted playfully and shrugged. An older woman was standing outside a window, looking in, slightly trembling, just a shadow through the murky glass. 'I have more in common with that poor woman than with anyone in here,' thought Clarissa.

Their drinks arrived. White Wine and a New York Sour. The waiter placed the glasses in front of them without asking who had which one. Clarissa expected Queenie would be handed the bill the same way.

'We both have a passion for past treasures and new ways of thinking,' Queenie carried on.

Clarissa shrugged. 'Who doesn't?'

Queenie pulled out a cigarette, lit it and inhaled the smoke. She looked around, content. 'But, you see, for most it is unfulfilled. We live it. We experience this,' indicating the scene with her hands, 'but we're so much more.'

'You do blend in very well. Apart from...' Clarissa reached out for the curious pendant.

Queenie's hand slid under the jacket first. She held up the pendant by its chain and swung it in front of Clarissa triumphantly.

'This? When did you spot it?'

'Spot it? You mean you were hiding it?'

'Why would I hide a pendant?'

'Exactly. Why?' Clarissa asked innocently.

The two women stared at each other. Putting the pendant away, Queenie had a sip of her cocktail. 'It's very valuable.'

'More so than your handbag?'

'My handbag has no value to me.'

Clarissa leant back on the chair, her eyes fixed on Queenie.

'Here's my dilemma: though not diamond this pendant could be fashion, for all I know. But it's cracked – so why doesn't she have it replaced? Or it has sentimental value; it could be an inheritance for instance. Why would she insist on carrying it when it's clearly going to break? Why wouldn't she keep grandma's fairytales and cherry pie smell home in a velvet-padded box, safely?' She pointed at Queenie's chest. 'That pendant bothers me.'

Queenie smiled and pointed back at Clarissa, playfully: 'There is a lot about Miss Miller that bothers me. Here is my dilemma: she turns up to a reading she clearly dislikes. She makes a sulky, half-spirited political protest to a crowd of girls who couldn't give a damn about it. Then she asks me to sign a book. A book I have never ever seen in my life. The title is mine all right. But that cover. Trust me I've checked all my book designs and it's not one of them.'

The two women stared at each other calmly. Then Clarissa burst out laughing.

'You're right. We do have a lot in common...' She admitted.

Queenie blew the smoke out triumphantly, her gaze focused on the firm bottom of the waiter walking past. To Clarissa's satisfaction he didn't even notice Queenie. As she followed Queenie's stare Clarissa saw the blurry outline of a woman through the unclean glass again. This time it seemed clearer; even familiar somehow. The table suddenly shook as a man reeled past and grabbed it for support. He ran his fingers through his white hair then touched the shocked Queenie's face. His eyes wide, clearly shaken, he made an effort to form words:

'Jess! Jessica, it's me, Harry.'

Queenie took a quick look at him then turned away, picking up her handbag and its contents off the bar floor.

'Her name isn't Jess,' said Clarissa gently to Harry, helping him regain balance. 'And she doesn't live here.'

'But I'm sure it is her,' the man whispered, as if afraid the illusion would escape him. 'Or her granddaughter...It's Harry.' He tried to explain again, leaning towards Queenie.

Clarissa shook her head: 'It must be a mistake. I'm sorry.' The man walked off slowly, looking back from time to time.

'What a creep, a stupid drunken jerk!' Queenie huffed, but her voice was trembling.

'Don't worry about it. He just mistook you for someone,' Clarissa couldn't help adding, mockingly, '...Jess.'

'Stop it!' Queenie was furious, but suddenly changed tone. 'Well, as I said, we both have a few hidden stories.'

'So you did know him?'

'I might have. That's why I wanted to talk to you. You look the kind who'd understand.'

'We can't talk here.'

'Why not? Even if they heard us, they wouldn't believe a word we say.'

'You have a whole team with you.' Clarissa pointed at one of the Sheikhs, getting a drink at the bar.

'Oh, I carry them around to distract the fans from me. They know nothing. They won't even notice we're leaving!' Queenie jumped up, grabbed Clarissa's hand and slid her other hand under her pearl jacket. 'Look,' she whispered to Clarissa as she pulled her up from the table.

The music seemed to have slowed down into one long note, gently waving and vibrating in the air. The waiter, carrying a glass of champagne on a tray above his head stopped mid-air, balancing on his toes like a ballerina. Harry, resting in an armchair was still staring at the empty spot Queenie had been sat in a moment ago. They were now weaving through the silent crowd, Queenie excited and Clarissa surprised, trying to figure out what shocked them so much as to make them stop in their tracks. Queenie grinned back at Clarissa, then stuffed a few dollar notes in a waiter's pocket as they passed him. While the force tipped him a little, he didn't seem to mind and neither did the cocktail in his hand – the glass moved but the liquid surface calmly sloped with it, refusing to regain horizontal position. This confirmed Clarissa's suspicion: either time had stopped for them, or Queenie and Clarissa's time had sped up. Either way, Queenie held the room in the stillness of a photograph...except for a figure moving quickly past the bar, casting a shadow on each hazy glass until it vanished from sight. Was it the same old woman she saw before? Clarissa felt Queenie's hand release the grip she held her with and slowly slide onto her waist. The much shorter Queenie was now facing her, dreamily staring up at Clarissa, holding her close with her hands and her eyes. 'Can I have the last dance?' she asked with a confident smile, leading Clarissa gently between the motionless bodies towards the exit in the large twirls of the Viennese Waltz.

'This has always been my favourite dance,' she whispered into Clarissa's ear, tiptoeing. Through the cloud of Chanel Clarissa caught the scent of Queenie's skin. 'Did you know it was a peasant dance? The noblemen found it absolutely filthy and outrageous. So it caught on.' Clarissa felt dizzy and maybe a little bit drunk. Queenie's hair was all ruffled up she seemed to have given herself over to the dance, spinning closer and closer to the axis, pulling Clarissa towards herself. Clarissa held on to Queenie's hand as they slowly swayed through the crowd, bumping into tables, chairs and people now entirely frozen in time but never overbalancing them, like ghosts dancing through the land of the living. They neared the entrance and to Clarissa's shock the windows that had revealed the moving silhouette of the elderly woman now showed the passers-by with one foot in the air, admiring the setting sun in silence.

They are heading to the station, thought the woman who had been watching them through the window. Wrapped in a warm scarf, battling icy wind and snow, she followed Queenie and Clarissa with her eyes. She reached out to touch the brickwork of the walls she hid behind but felt nothing. *Not yet.*

'It's a bit of a walk,' said Clarissa. She felt uneasy. Queenie seemed too excited, singing and skipping along. She looked about twenty-three. People say the eyes never change but they must do: Clarissa saw in Queenie's eyes the sort of joy and love of life that only comes to one with time. 'How old are you really?' she asked.

'Well I won't tell you that but people do wonder how I kept my looks all these years...,' Queenie leant to Clarissa and lowered her voice. 'I tell them it's the cigarettes but I think you and I know the real reason.' She lifted her pendant and swung it in front of her as if she was trying to put her under hypnosis. 'Pure radium!' she whispered. 'If people knew they'd kill for this.' She took off her pendant entirely and held it out to Clarissa. 'Try it! You'll feel the difference.'

Clarissa tried to remain calm. *This cannot be radium. It wouldn't make her young. She's testing me.* She snatched the pendant away from Queenie and closed her palm around it. 'It feels great.' She was trying to see if she could stop time like Queenie did, but Queenie forced her fist open and retrieved the pendant. 'I better look after it. As you can imagine, it was hard to acquire,' she said with a wink.

There isn't much time left. I need to act soon, the woman thought, trying to rush from corner to corner to keep up with them, while still hidden. She held out her hand to gently rattle the iron fencing of the factory she was passing. The cold, heavy metal barely moved.

The last of the evening's sunshine gave a strange glow to the station. It looked lonely, magical and very fragile. Clarissa's heart grew heavy. She realised she was bringing danger home. What made her even sadder is that Queenie was a good companion. Coming across people like that in their isolated adventures reminded Clarissa of her loneliness.

'What a gloomy building!' Queenie broke the silence. They approached the building by the back door as Clarissa was tired of explaining why she lived at a police station.

'We don't need to go in,' Clarissa offered, relieved.

'I love gloom,' said Queenie as she pushed past Clarissa and opened the door.

Inside, she stopped Clarissa on the corridor. 'I'd normally be out of here by now, you know,' she whispered. 'I stop time, find the power source, top up my pendant and am miles down the road when I release you. But something's different tonight. I took a risk, because...' She bit her nail nervously. 'I want you to come with me.'

'You're doing what with the pendant?' Despite her shock Clarissa felt she knew all along this was coming. In fact, it made sense. The radio went silent not because Queenie was in the area but because Clarissa was going to bring her to the station and help her take away its energy. Without that, the station would be an ordinary building, and the radio an ordinary receiver with no signals bleeding back from the future.

'It's running out of power. I need to harvest some energy. But the point is, you should join me.'

'Why should I do that?' Clarissa asked, lightly. 'Maybe I'm happy here,' she said, trying to gain time. Under the circumstances, she thought, rather irritated, I run out of time way too often.

Queenie let out a triumphant giggle: 'Well then, if it's so great why don't you show me around?'

Clarissa scratched her head and walked past Queenie, up to the door ahead, then turned back. 'There's other people living here, you see...'

'I know. I can tell you travel in a community. With men.' She smirked.

Clarissa was afraid of opening the door. She didn't want to see her friends frozen and helpless. 'Have you stopped time?' she asked quietly.

'I used up all my energy... our energy at the bar. It won't work now.'

'You used it up for that? Why?'

Queenie looked amused. 'Didn't it work?' Then, more gravely, she added: 'You don't like risking everything, do you? I do it all the time.'

'Witty.' Clarissa carefully opened the door.

Dogberry and Whitney were playing poker, staring at their cards. Clarissa's heart sank for the split second before they looked up, slammed down their hands and skipped to their feet. Their anxiety took Clarissa by surprise. Glancing back she understood why: Queenie was holding a gun at them, while still adjusting her stocking where she must have kept it before.

'There's no need for that,' Clarissa said calmly.

'Because you're coming with me? Or because you're happy for me to take the station's energy? I like you, girl. But I don't trust you.'

'You're not very trustworthy yourself. Not very responsible.'

'Stay where you are!' shouted Queenie as Whitney tried to move. 'Or I'll shoot you!' Whitney held his hand up. Queenie turned back to Clarissa.

'After a couple of centuries you lose sympathy for people who won't make their own luck.'

Noticing the third cup of tea and a folded hand on the table, she spun around. 'Where's the third one?'

As if cued, Wilson entered the room, whistling an upbeat song. Halfway to the table he noticed the situation and froze. Queenie skipped over to him, grabbed his shoulder and held the gun to his head.

'You were hiding the prettiest one!' she grinned, holding on to Wilson.

'You love a handsome man, don't you?' snapped Clarissa, irritated. 'Why would you want me to come with you? We are so different...'

'You remind me of my younger self. With the discipline, responsibility and dreams your age has. Just spending this evening with you felt so reinvigorating, I nearly want to save the world again. You're having a good effect on me. Maybe if we were to travel together you could make me into a better girl. We could live the high-life, go to all the best parties, mix with the best of whatever society we end up in and stay young forever. What is there to even think about? Just tell me where the power source is and we can start a new life.'

'Look, I want to come but I genuinely don't know.'

'You don't know? Do you think it's that easy?'

'If I may...' began Dogberry.

'No, you may not!' Queenie shook the gun at him, still holding Wilson.

'Are we in this together?' she asked Clarissa while holding the gun at Wilson's temple.

'I'm coming with you. I told you already.'

'It's time you proved it – I've been open with you tonight, so don't hold out on me.' Was it her anger powering up the pendant again, wondered Clarissa, as she spotted bright sparks appearing under Queenie's jacket. Queenie carried on, shouting and shaking the gun.

'Living in your little shell, thinking you're above us all! You go out there and live in the world like I do for a while, then tell us to work ten hours a day, toil away in a damn factory for a pittance just to prove a fucking point!' She mimicked Clarissa. 'It's more important than dancing and having fun! But I guess you are cosier here, I guess you'd rather make speeches about how everyone should live than to actually live yourself.'

From the corner of her eye, through the window Clarissa caught sight of the same silhouette she saw earlier. This time it was clearer, and somehow very bright, with the same sparks as Queenie's pendant - perhaps reflecting the last rays of the sun.

'Calm down, Queenie.' Clarissa said gently. 'Let Wilson go.'

'You're right. He's not the one stopping me,' said Queenie. Still holding Wilson she now aimed the gun at Clarissa.

Before Queenie could fire, the lights flickered and went out. The front door opened with a gust of cold wind and, to everyone's surprise, a few snowflakes floated in. Then, in the darkness of dusk appeared a brightly glowing figure.

The sight of this other worldly creature, shaking snow from her hair and reaching out towards Queenie with red, frozen fingers bid everyone still. A twisting, sparkling coil of energy elevated her from the ground, pushing her towards the shocked Queenie. Or, rather, towards Queenie's pendant that was the white of burning magnesium, its tentacle-like sparks reaching towards the flames that carried what was now identified by everyone as an elderly lady wrapped in a thick coat and scarf.

Reaching her, the mysterious woman twisted the gun out of Queenie's hand. The group looked on in amazement. Sparks began to spit and space swirled around Queenie's pendant. The pair now lost their original shapes and their arms and legs followed the whirls of energy. Linked into each other's arms, fighting, delivering punches they spun around, pulled by a higher energy, struggling to find footing like dancers unsure of their steps.

'Quick!' shouted Dogberry. 'Help her!' As the team approached the pair, they could see their own arms and legs bending and shrinking, fading and popping up again in bright colours. They gurgled in surprise while following the odd creatures floating towards the entrance, still twirling slowly. As they reached the door everyone's form took up a more traditional human shape, with a less controversial choice on limb length and width. Queenie sat down on the ground, rubbing her forehead.

'What just happened?'

The stranger, who looked eerily like an older version of Clarissa, grabbed Queenie by her shoulders and shook her. 'You tramp, you blew up the station trying to suck its energy up with that knackered old necklace and killed all of them but me! And you would have done it again if I hadn't stopped you!' As she was speaking, she was growing fainter, more indistinct.

Wilson turned to Clarissa: 'Is this your auntie?'

Clarissa shook her head, speechless.

The lady was now fading away quickly. She smiled, and this time they could hear her clearly: 'I missed this station. And I missed you lot, though the silly cow was right about...' she couldn't say anything more as her silhouette faded and she vanished.

'It was me... she was me...' said Clarissa, pondering. 'But where did she go? And where is Queenie?'

'Yes!'

They turned at Queenie's cry of triumph, and saw her holding the pendant that the older Clarissa had brought back with her. Before anyone could stop her she whipped it onto her neck alongside the one she was already wearing. It hissed and cracked, reminding Clarissa of the famous Tesla coil she saw at one of the world exhibitions. 'It's picking up energy! I'm young for another century!' she announced as the flames reached her dress. In a flash, the pendants exploded.

The group ducked as the explosion threw Queenie's charred handbag towards them. Except for Clarissa, who was already crouching, still feeling the ground where her older self stood a minute ago. 'She's gone... Where has she gone?' she murmured. She looked up at Dogberry, who was dusting himself and examining the handbag. 'What did she mean by 'she was right about'?'

'We'll probably never know. Maybe you were happy living outside the station,' said Whitney.

'Or about the importance of staying young!' guessed Wilson from the window, examining the spot where Queenie exploded.

Clarissa stood up and dusted herself. 'Never mind. But I do wonder where I disappeared to.'

'Hard to say,' murmured Dogberry as if he was talking to himself, while struggling to undo the brass clasp on the purse. 'Perhaps, having undone the action that led to her version of the future she's ceased to exist. Or perhaps she's been jolted into her own life again, like a train switching onto a different track before jumping back.'

'Involving another dimension of some sort, I dare say,' added Wilson.

They all turned to Dogberry to confirm the idea, but Dogberry wasn't listening any more. He had found a crossword puzzle in Queenie's handbag.

The Mystery of the Drowned Bird

Eddie Robson

'I'm popping down to the kitchen,' says Kenny Kelly. 'I might be some time.'

Jay has rolled him a joint to see him through the journey, and he hands this to Kenny now. Suzie has written everyone's orders for food and drink down on a cigarette paper: she licks the paper and sticks it to the back of Kenny's left hand. Kenny sets his guitar aside and, unsteadily, clambers to his feet. Ben moves the guitar, because Kenny is about to stand on the neck and break it. And Kenny turns and leaves the room.

Kenny has lived at Dedekind House for a year. The house is over two hundred years old, and was designed for a family and a complement of servants. Kenny has no family – luckily, his divorce came through just before the sale did – and even if he wanted to employ house staff, such a thing would be out of the question for a man like him at this moment in history. The house is much too big for a man living alone, but Kenny likes to feel the space around him. In eight years with his band, The Lazy Eyes, he has grown accustomed to hotel rooms, buses, aeroplanes; to endless hours staring at the walls of Olympic Studios, performing take after take; to being jostled and crowded everywhere he goes in public. At Dedekind he feels he can finally spread out. He never hears anyone except his guests, and sometimes not even them. On the evening of New

Year's Day he was startled to happen upon Steve Winwood working on some lyrics in the library, having assumed Steve had left before lunch.

The journey from lounge to kitchen involves walking one hundred and two yards down the corridor, descending the stairs into the hallway, proceeding to the stairs next to the front door and descending those, then going all the way to the back of the house, where the kitchen is located. The journey takes around three minutes if one walks briskly. Kenny never walks briskly.

Kenny descends the steps into the hallway and walks to the front door. As he does so, the telephone begins to ring. Kenny ignores it. It's after two o'clock in the morning, so the call must be from his brother William, The Lazy Eyes' bass player. William is concerned that Kenny has had no contact with the rest of the group since not bothering to attend the last couple of mixing sessions for their new album, four months ago. Is Kenny still a member of the group, William will want to know? Well, thinks Kenny as he enters the kitchen, brews another pot of tea and grabs some beers, I haven't decided that myself yet.

Kenny could just fancy some chocolates right now. He got loads for Christmas, but fucking Clapton ate them all.

The joint has gone out. Kenny re-lights it, puts all the food and drink on a tray and heads back through the passage and up to the front door, through the hallway, past the police station and up the –

Two steps up, Kenny turns.

The police station which fills the hallway, and was not there five minutes ago, is a concretey, flat-roofed, two-storey affair. The word POLICE is written in large, unfriendly letters on an illuminated sign above the door, casting its cold blue light over everything in the darkened hallway. Kenny can see nobody inside.

Kenny's mouth hangs open. His joint falls into Ben's scotch and coke.

A light goes on in the police station, just behind the door. Behind the glass, a murky shape moves.

Kenny drops the tray. The teapot shatters, its contents spilling across the steps — but none of the scalding liquid touches Kenny, because he is already fleeing up the stairs.

The door of the police station opens and Constable Wilson emerges into Dedekind House. He hears the last echoes of someone else's footsteps, but is too late to tell where they went. Wilson glances back at the station, taking in its unprepossessing appearance. Materialising inside a house? It's never done that before. Maybe he did something wrong. Maybe he shouldn't have travelled on his own. It was a momentary whim: he was staying late at the station to catch up on some paperwork and, in a fit of boredom, decided to take a trip.

From where Wilson stands the house seems at least as big as Manleigh Hall, which he has had the privilege of visiting several times. It's a very different sort of place though, even Wilson can see that and he's no expert: fixtures such as the staircase are more ornate than Manleigh Hall's, and the layout is not symmetrical.

Wilson kneels beside the shattered contents of the tea-tray. Steam rises from the soaked carpet into the cold air of the hallway. He knows that the year is 1970: clearly it's also winter. Through the window of the station, Wilson caught a glimpse of a man – bearded, long-haired. The man can't possibly be the master of the house, nor can he be staff. The place has intruders. But intruders who make tea for themselves?

Wilson rises, walks up the stairs and makes a fifty-fifty guess about which way down the corridor he should go. The route takes him towards a summer room with a swimming pool, which runs the entire height of the house. Access from the upper storey is via a balcony which has been extended and had an attractive spiral staircase added, allowing one to descend to the poolside area below.

It is from this balcony that Wilson observes the body which lies in the swimming pool. A large, colourful fur-lined coat and long, dark hair spread across the surface of the water, offering small but sadly unmistakable hints of a human form underneath.

Wilson reacts. He descends the spiral staircase, almost tripping on the iron steps as he hurtles downwards. He arrives at the edge of the pool and, although he can't swim, considers diving in. But as the echo of his footsteps dies away, the stillness of the large room strikes him, and the stillness of the body at its centre.

The lady is dead.

Wilson removes his hat and nods respectfully in her direction. He then performs a circuit of the crime scene, sometimes stopping to crouch and observe it from a different angle, like a snooker player considering an awkward shot. He returns to the top of the staircase and looks down. He makes notes in his little notebook. Then he flips the notebook closed, replaces it in his pocket and purposefully walks back into the main house.

Kenny has agitatedly assured his guests that he has taken no LSD tonight whatsoever, and there genuinely is a police station in the downstairs hallway. His guests are sceptical, and all suspect each other of spiking their host. None of them take him seriously enough even to check. However, everyone has grudgingly decided to humour him in case he turns violent, like he did that time when his brother was here.

Everyone been dispatched to various corners of the house to fetch every stash of drugs Kenny can recall the location of. They have tracked down marijuana, amphetamines, LSD and cocaine, and all have vanished down the toilet in the bathroom between the two master bedrooms. Everyone except Kenny was very upset to see it all go. They have done a thorough job, too: the only drugs now left in the house reside in a joint which Jay pocketed whilst Kenny wasn't looking, and which Kenny still does not know about.

On Kenny's instructions, they are trying to 'act natural'. The hitch is that for the assembled company, 'acting natural' consists of loafing around taking drugs.

At this point it finally occurs to one of them – Suzie, as it happens – to ask, 'Where's Caroline?'

And nobody can think of an answer.

Just then, footsteps approach from down the hallway. Heavy footsteps. Unmistakably policeman's footsteps.

Everyone except Kenny is incredulous when Wilson steps through the open door. He is tall, fresh-faced, has a bit of a swagger about him: the old-fashioned style of his uniform does not go unnoticed.

Wilson stands in the doorway, looking at everyone in turn, looking them up and down. Kenny: skinny, bad teeth, cream-coloured shirt and brown corduroy suit. Jay: well-built, curly hair, T-shirt and fisherman's sweater, all of which needs washing. Suzie: blonde, slim, hard-featured, kaftan, leather jacket, a camera hanging from her left hand by its strap. Ben: African-American, tall, imposing, dressed in a frill-fronted suit.

Wilson is giving them a look he has practised, designed to make them think that he knows everything. On most people it works well.

Kenny and his guests wait for Wilson to speak. He does not.

'Can I...' says Kenny, his mouth drying. He swallows. 'Can I help you, officer?'

Wilson gets out his notebook, flips it open and reads. 'Young lady in a brightly coloured coat – rainbow colours. Long black hair. Probably about five foot nine, five ten... black boots.' He looks up. 'Ring any bells?'

The others all look at each other. 'Caroline?' says Suzie.

Wilson writes down 'Caroline'. Then he looks up again. 'She's dead.'

Wilson sits in a sumptuously-upholstered armchair and rules out four pages in his notebook, one for each suspect. It's clear to him that foul play is involved somewhere: people don't just fall into swimming pools fully clothed and drown. The water is only five feet deep. There's nothing she could have knocked herself unconscious on. What was she doing near the pool on her own anyway? None of it makes sense. Something happened here.

Assuming nobody else entered the house tonight – and all the doors are locked, and there is no sign of forced entry – one of the four he spoke to is the culprit. Wilson just needs to look for motive and opportunity.

He calls for his first interviewee.

The first few minutes of Kenny's interview are spent convincing Wilson that he is indeed the house's owner, and that the house has no staff. Kenny is deeply alarmed by Caroline's death, but also relieved that Wilson has not even mentioned drugs.

Wilson finally seems to accept Kenny as the man of the house. Then he asks, 'And your name is?'

Kenny lets out a short laugh, then realises Wilson is serious, and this raises a further source of unease. Although Kenny affects to be in retreat, he still buys Record Mirror, NME, Melody Maker and Disc & Music Echo every week and, when nobody's around, scours the news pages of each, partly to find out what his rivals are up to, but mostly to read speculation about himself. Initially he found suggestions of an imminent Lazy Eyes split ('LAZY EYES GOING IN DIFFERENT DIRECTIONS?'), with a Kenny Kelly solo album rumoured to be already on Booker Records' schedule for 1970. However, over the course of the last four months, whilst stories about The Lazy Eyes have continued, Kenny has been mentioned less and less. Increasingly he would find his name noted only in the penultimate paragraph. Journalists seem to have stopped asking the other members of the band about him. Most worryingly, Kenny has not featured in any of the end-of-year round-ups, nor the start-of-the-year previews.

At first he put it down to a ploy on the part of Ian, their manager. Trying to make him see he wasn't indispensable. But if Ian could control press coverage like that, a lot of pieces about the group would never have appeared.

So, why then?

'Kenny Kelly,' he tells Wilson. And Kenny tells himself, it doesn't mean anything if a copper doesn't recognise him. The guy's a square.

Wilson writes his name down on his notepad. 'Occupation?'

'Musician.'

Wilson writes this down and adds a question mark. 'And the deceased... Caroline?'

'I didn't really know her,' Kenny says, too quickly. 'Ben brought her.'

Wilson points his pen in the direction of the next room. 'The negro gentleman?'

Kenny wants to challenge the copper's phrase, but hesitates – he doesn't want to piss the guy off – and the moment passes. 'She seemed a nice sort of bird.'

'What was her surname?'

'Don't think anyone said it.'

'Was she married?'

'Don't think so.' Is she – was she – Ben's girlfriend? He isn't sure, and he doesn't want to drop Ben in it. And don't mention Ben's a draft-dodger, whatever you do don't mention that.

'So. Can you give me your account of events this evening?'

Once Kenny has finished, it's Jay's turn. It is possibly the most awful experience of Jay's life. He stares at the copper, talking, talking, barely able to remember anything he says. He describes things in too much detail, he rambles, he digresses. He can see he's annoying the copper but he can't stop. He just wants the guy to say, That's all, you can go.

Jay needs something to calm himself down. He reaches into his pocket, pulls out a cigarette. 'Do you mind if I smoke?'

'Yes,' says Wilson. But in his muddled nervousness Jay hears 'No,' and starts lighting the cigarette anyway. Before the lighter touches the end, Wilson leans forward and says 'Yes, I do mind,' and Jay sheepishly puts the lighter away again, in the knowledge that he's just made things worse.

It's only when he removes the cigarette from his mouth that he realises it's not a cigarette, and he almost lit the joint he's been carrying. Christ almighty. The copper doesn't seem to have noticed. Jay puts it back in his pocket and goes on talking, even less coherently than before.

Suzie is by the pool. Suzie wonders why the copper doesn't have anyone else with him to fish poor Caroline out. Then again, she also wonders why the copper's police station is inside Kenny's house. She saw it in the hallway whilst walking here, and was tempted to take a picture, but nobody would believe it was real.

Suzie goes down on one knee by the side of the pool, and for a moment seems to be paying her respects. Then she raises her camera and snaps away.

The last time she offered some shots of Kenny's house to the press, she didn't get a single bite. That had been after his birthday party in November. She's still fucked off about that: they're good shots, the best work she did all last year. Why didn't they want them?

Kenny liked them. He had one blown up and gave it to his mother for Christmas.

Suzie hopes taking pictures of Caroline doesn't spoil her friendship with Kenny... but if it does, so be it. If she passes up this opportunity, she's no kind of journalist at all. Pretty dead girl in a rock star's swimming pool. (You can't see she's pretty in these pictures, but Suzie has several from earlier in the evening where you can).

Suzie walks halfway up the spiral stairs and takes some shots from there. Up on the balcony, the door opens and Suzie jumps. She walks to the top of the steps and finds Jay there.

'What are you doing?' says Jay, looking not at Suzie but at the body. Then he glances down at the camera. 'Oh Suze, you didn't?'

'Of course I did.'

'Poor Caroline... I think the copper thinks I did it.'

'What? But it must have been an accident, surely?'

'Well probably.'

'She was hammered.'

'Yeah of course, but we can't say that, can we? Kenny's in line for a bust – ever since he bought this house. When one of us lot starts playing at lords and ladies, they don't like it. They'll take him down a peg. I knew I shouldn't have come here...' Jay also knows that the first thing he should have done after getting out of the interview was get rid of the joint before the copper finds it. He should have done that before the interview. He can't understand why he hasn't. But then Suzie's voice breaks this train of thought.

'She was tripping. Probably didn't know where she

was, probably thought the water was... fucking... outer space or something.' She sighs. 'It's all of our fault.'

'What?'

'We knew what she'd taken. We shouldn't have let her go off alone.'

Unfamiliar words and phrases swirl around Wilson's notebook: roadie, which is what Jay was before he became a road manager for a mod band called The Tourniquets, who have split up and whose guitarist has formed a heavy soul supergroup with Ben, called Cruise Control. The woman Suzie, who is a photographer for the rock press, is here to take pictures of Ben for an article.

Wilson needs to find a clue somewhere in all this, and is convinced he will find it somewhere in the connections between these people. He is currently interviewing Ben, who was the one who brought the chick (meaning Caroline) to the house. 'Just someone I met at a gig,' Ben says when Wilson asks him how he knew the deceased. 'She only seemed interested in Kenny.'

'Interested how?' Wilson says.

'A fan, I guess. She was way excited when I told her I knew him. I figured he'd like to meet her.'

'Why?'

'She was cute. And last time I was here, Kenny was saying about how fans never came up to the house any more. Thought I'd bring one to him.' He names her as Caroline Austin, and thinks he last saw her alive 'around midnight, I guess.' Like the others, he does not remember exactly when or why Miss Austin left the room. Ben's explanation of the failure to query her prolonged absence: 'People do their own thing here.'

'Own thing?' asks Wilson.

'Sure. If people wanna go into another room to crash, or hook up, they go.'

Wilson taps his pad with his pencil. 'All right, that's all for now.'

Ben stands and walks from the room.

The evidence is not stacking up well. Wilson expected the interviews to expose tensions within the group. With suspicion hanging over them all, he expected them to deflect it onto each other by speculating how and why the others might have done it. But they have all confirmed that none of them left the room until Kenny went to fetch tea... and Wilson has seen the evidence that Kenny did fetch tea. Consulting his notes, Wilson sees that Jay remembers putting a phonographic record on to play immediately after Kenny left the room: Wilson has the record beside him (the title, which he writes down, is Crosby, Stills & Nash). Using this they have established that Kenny was not gone for more than ten minutes. Wilson intends to test whether it is possible to go from here to the swimming pool, drown a woman, then go to the kitchen, make a pot of tea, and return in that time: but he doubts it.

Wilson knows he is missing something. He will have to think harder.

But first, he's going to take a break and go for a piss.

Emerging into the hallway, Wilson sees Suzie and Jay approaching from the other direction.

'Are you ready for me?' asks Suzie, coolly.

Wilson points in the direction from which they just came. 'Have you just come from the swimming pool?'

Jay points at Suzie and says quickly, 'She was in there, I went to get her, that's the only reason I was in there.'

Suzie glares at Jay.

'And why were you in there?' Wilson asks Suzie.

Suzie holds up her camera. 'Taking pictures.'

'Why?'

'That's my job.'

'So you must think you can make money from them.'

'Well. Yeah, but...' And then Suzie notices what Jay's doing: he's preparing to light a joint. In front of the copper. She just stares for a moment, unable to believe what she sees. Then she kicks his foot. 'Jay...' she hisses.

Jay looks up, genuinely surprised. 'What are you kicking me for?'

Wilson plucks the joint from Jay's lips before it fully lights. The paper at the very end glows, but this dies in a second. 'I told you. No smoking. I don't like getting it in my mouth. All right?' Then he turns on his heel and goes to find Kenny.

Kenny is in the other room with Ben. The atmosphere has gone flat. Lacking any kind of social lubricant –

they're too nervous even to drink alcohol – they sit in silence.

The policeman's head bobs around the frame of the door. 'Toilet?'

Kenny and Ben share a glance of concern, which both of them immediately hope isn't noticed by Wilson.

'Keep going, third door on the left,' says Kenny.

Wilson nods his thanks and departs, leaving Kenny to clench his fingers against his sweaty palms. Kenny is pretty sure he didn't drop anything when he was rushing to the toilet to flush it all. But then, he was in a hurry.

Wilson stands behind the locked door and relieves himself. It occurs to him that he hasn't been offered a cup of tea since arriving here. That won't do them any favours.

He thinks over the facts as he knows them. The woman's photography is an intriguing development (ha ha! he thinks. No pun intended). Is she set to benefit from what has happened here? How much? Is it worth killing for? It depends on the context, which Wilson knows he lacks.

Wilson tosses the cigarette he took from Jay into the toilet bowl, flushes, washes his hands, dries them (nice thick hand towel), unlocks the door and leaves the bathroom.

He's gone no more than ten paces down the hallway when he hears the noise from behind him. He feels it, too: a combination of a rumble and a gurgle.

A splash of water comes over the top of the toilet bowl and spills onto the carpet. The bloody thing must be blocked. Well, he's damned if he's fixing it.

Then a slosh of water comes from the bowl. Then another. They hit the floor, noisily. The water that's coming up is clean. Eventually the noise summons Kenny, followed by Ben.

'Fucking hell,' says Kenny. 'What did you do?'

'Oi!' says Wilson. 'Don't talk to an officer of the law like that.'

In the bathroom, the lurches of water up from the toilet bowl are becoming more violent.

'Should we call somebody?' says Ben.

The three of them are joined by Suzie and Jay. 'What did you do?' asks Suzie.

'Nothing!' says Wilson.

And then the toilet bowl splits open. A diagonal crack runs across it in the blink of an eye and the pieces fall to the floor, thudding on the wet carpet.

And then the drugs come pouring out. Mostly marijuana, but also a scattering of undissolved pills, soggy tabs of acid and clumps of white powder.

The flow of water has abated. The noise has gone. The evidence that damns Kenny and his guests lies across the floor. They wait for a reaction from Wilson, but Wilson has no idea what he's looking at.

Then the drugs catch fire. This should be impossible: the floor is sodden.

Wilson turns back to the others. 'You need to tell me what's going on here, right now.'

But he stares into four blank faces. They don't know. Whatever secret they've been keeping from him, this is not it.

He turns back to the bathroom. The flames are growing out of all proportion to the material being burned. The fire starts to catch the door, which draws a weak protest from Kenny. But they all realise something much worse is happening.

The flames burst along the corridor, and in seconds the floor, the walls, the ceiling are all ablaze. Sam is first to try to run – but the fire has obscured the corridor's turnings, in both directions. 'There's no way out!' he tells the others.

Wilson's nervous companions are terrified, but he trusts all his senses equally: the fire is not hot. It's just light. It won't harm them. Wilson takes a deep breath to calm himself.

And gets a lungful of smoke.

The smoke clears, and Wilson is elsewhere. A gaudy red room containing two chairs. On one of the chairs, Wilson sits. On the other chair sits a creature whose form is unclear – it seems larger than the space it occupies, it seems strong, it seems beautiful, and yet if he looks properly it's nothing more than a cloud of smoke. Wilson feels his emotions surge in the creature's presence – he feels impressed, humbled, flattered.

'Am I here to interview you?' Wilson asks.

Yes, the creature replies, and adds that it likes being interviewed.

'Who are you?'

Its name is The Eminence.

'What do you want?'

It came here to feed on Kenny's fame.

'Fame? I don't understand.'

It has been hiding in Kenny's marijuana and the idiot sets fire to it himself so he never suspects a thing: that's usually the tricky part, making sure its victims don't notice the smoke going in. It has enjoyed the luxury of supping slowly at Kenny's fame, taking a little at a time. It planned to keep this going until the summer – by which point Kenny would have forgotten his own name and been left a gibbering wreck – but then Caroline came. She did well to find it, and to get into the house – but she didn't know what form the creature took, and she had smoked the joints that went around so as to seem inconspicuous. So it got inside her brain and dealt with her. And now here is Wilson, on Caroline's trail.

'I didn't come here to –'

The Eminence is not interested in Wilson's denials. Given the way he arrived here, and within an hour of Caroline's death too, he must be a colleague of hers. Damned Tangential Detectives always catch up with you in the end. Wilson's tactics were clever. His appearance was so sudden, so surprising, that Kenny almost disposed of every drug in the house before the Eminence could stop him. It tried to get inside Wilson more subtly, by influencing Jay... still hoping Kenny would be left unsuspecting and available to feed on. But now it has been forced to take more dramatic measures.

'What are you going to do?'

It will drain Wilson, and then the other four, and then it will leave.

And now Wilson feels a different surge of emotions.

The red room has disappeared while Wilson wasn't looking, and the smoke has enveloped him completely. All he can see is smoke. He feels the Eminence take a grip on his sense of self. Then it starts to rattle him. It pulls on all Wilson's certainties and shrouds them in doubt. It shows him who he is and then twists this image, then again, then again, showing him from multiple subjective viewpoints. It takes hold of the rug of Wilson's beliefs and tries to tug it away.

But to its surprise, the metaphorical rug will not budge.

The Eminence tries harder. But it is just starting to realise that Wilson's belief in truth is uncommonly strong. Kenny was easy prey – an inflated ego, grown fragile by exposure to psychedelics and the paranoia that followed in the wake of his success. Wilson has no paranoia. He trusts his judgement, he trusts what he knows. The recent broadening of his horizons has not altered this. He accepts these things, he approaches them rationally: as he has faced these challenges, he has only become more confident.

The Eminence tries harder. It picks at his fears, his inadequacies. It echoes them back to him, amplified, exaggerated.

But Wilson knows these things already. He has the measure of himself. He cannot be undermined this way.

The Eminence wraps itself around Wilson's psyche... tighter... tighter...

And Wilson puts it to the back of his mind, to think about later.

Wilson opens his eyes. He is still in the corridor, but there's no trace of a fire: the wallpaper is unscathed. The substances which floated back up out of the toilet have vanished. The toilet bowl is still broken, however, and the bathroom carpet is ruined.

Wilson looks down at the floor. There, Kenny and his guests emerge from the cringing, cowering heap into which they have gathered themselves. They stand up and look around.

'Shit,' says Ben to Kenny. 'Who sold you that stuff?'

Jay and Ben help Wilson to retrieve Caroline's body from the pool. During his contact with the Eminence, Wilson learned where she came from and he will take her back there. That will be tidier for everyone concerned. He will log the incident at Manleigh Halt. He likes writing the reports. Especially when Miss Miller helps (although she always wants to add bits to 'spice it up').

Caroline's associates will also, he hopes, be able to help him deal with the Eminence in his mind.

Kenny has found a sheet of wood in the cellar, large enough to lay the body out on. Wilson prepares to lift one end, but Suzie stops him. For a moment he thinks she wants to take a photograph. But instead, she crouches down and puts her hand under a corner, then indicates for the other three to follow suit.

Kenny, Jay, Suzie and Ben pick up Caroline's body and lift it, as silently as they can. Letting Wilson lead them, they carry it through the house. The first light of day touches them through the windows. Arriving in the hallway, they place Caroline inside the door of the police station.

'Thank you,' Wilson says.

'No, man – thank you,' says Kenny. None of them queried Wilson's explanation of what had happened. None of them feel in the mood to query anything. They only hope that it is, indeed, over.

Wilson goes to shake Kenny's hand. The other man draws Wilson into a warm embrace, which he holds for several seconds. 'Thank fuck for that,' Kenny says, then finally releases Wilson, who is too shocked to react. 'Anything I can ever do for you, mate. Anything.'

Wilson nods, bids farewell to all the others, then enters the police station and closes the door. Moments later, the station blinks out of existence with an ethereal sighing sound, leaving not even a crease in the carpet.

The four of them repair to the kitchen, where they eat toast and drink coffee with a dash of nerve-steadying bourbon. Jay offers to drive Ben and Suzie back to London. He makes this offer to Kenny, too.

'Cheers,' says Kenny. 'Think I'll stick here though.'

'You sure?' says Jay. 'I don't know if I'd want to be alone here, after that.'

'Yeah, no. I should call someone in to look at the bathroom.'

Ben says he'll put Kenny on the guest list for tomorrow night's gig at the Bag O'Nails. Suzie opens up her camera and hands Kenny the film. Then they depart, and Kenny is left at the kitchen table with his thoughts.

Before long, he stands up and makes the journey through the passage that runs under the house. He emerges from the stairway that comes up by the front door, where the telephone is. There's a Melody Maker in the wastebasket next to the telephone. Kenny fishes it out and turns its pages until he finds a phone number on the editorial page. He picks up the telephone and dials the number.

His call is answered.

'Hello?' says Kenny. 'It's Kenny Kelly here. I've got a story for you. About the future of The Lazy Eyes.'

His words provoke some scepticism, but also excitement. Is this really Kenny Kelly? What's the story?

'One thing first,' Kenny says: 'this will be front page news, won't it?'

Tilting at Windmills
Nick Mellish

There are few things in life more comforting than shelter, mused Sergeant Whitney. Warm, enveloping shelter which smothers you. Right now for example it was raining outside, the wind howling, but he was protected, sat by the bar in the Balmy Badger pub. A small fire burnt in one corner, its warmth covering tables round which card games were played, Monopoly was lost, the world was put to rights, and people sat in silence, listening to the weather, hoping it wouldn't be as bad as the great storm a few weeks ago which had so injured Sussex.

'It's not another hurricane,' came the repeated assertion.

Whitney had been in Lewes now for over a month, helping where possible to aid people as they struggled to get things back to normal. When the hurricane hit it had surprised and devastated so much and so many. It was why, Whitney reasoned, the good people of Manleigh Halt had arrived in 1987 in the first place: there was trouble, it was their job to fix it. Or his job, perhaps, as the others had travelled up North to investigate a crime scene where a teenager caught red-handed claimed that she had been temporarily possessed by the spirit of a supposedly missing horse named Shergar. The police were dismissing it as nonsense, but Whitney knew better than to do such things off-hand - a stray sugar lump in a back pocket could be the key to the crime. He also knew that staying put in Lewes to help tidy up had been a very good move indeed and now the cleaning was done, Whitney found himself growing comfortable.

The Balmy Badger helped: a nice bed, good food, good beer, good company. Either side of him sat people, almost friends: to his left was the head of the local Amateur Dramatics society, a timid bespectacled man called David, and to his right sat a colourful man with equally colourful language he knew only as Hopper, a rather nasty nickname that had stuck from school thanks to his club foot. He spent his days cleaning the streets, emptying bins, washing his hands, but as dustbin men went (and, in truth, Whitney was not certain how they went) he was pretty content.

Whitney stretched out like a cat. This almost felt like home.

'But of course,' Whitney had found himself saying a few days ago, 'the thing about travelling for as long as I have is that a sense of home becomes the people around you. It's less about the rooms you work or sleep in.'

'Travel, eh?' a voice had perked up. 'You're not one of those gypos, are you?'

Whitney had not mentioned his life to anyone else after that. Looking around now, he could see the owner of that voice; it belonged to Jeremy Symms, a local

Banker and an almost permanently irritated — and, these days, drunk - man. In fairness to him, life was pretty bad at present. He was leaving his wife, years of nagging and unreasonable behaviour having brought him to this point, or so he claimed. His wife told a slightly different version of events, one in which she was leaving him after years of verbal abuse, terrifyingly angry outbursts and cigarette burns all over the furniture. Whitney had dealt with people like him all his working life — men who thought they had their lives nailed down, only to find it slip out from under them. Most of them had landed back-side first in a pint glass, shouting the odds about the injustices of the world, unable to accept any responsibility for their own downfalls.

Music slipped through the cracks in conversations; at least he thought it was supposed to be music. Something about someone always being on someone's mind. He took another pull on his pint and smiled at Debbie, the landlady. She smiled back, all happy and warm, her deer-like eyes lighting up as she did so. Whitney looked away, a little embarrassed that such a person would smile like that to him. He shook away such thoughts and drank some more, feeling time ebb away.

Things were, of course, far too nice to last.

It was early the next day that there came a knock on Whitney's door. When he opened it, he was greeted by Debbie, her dark brown hair a mess of hurry and worry.

He could tell from the look on her pale face that something terrible had happened.

They took a brisk walk, turning corners and ducking down twittens, until they reached the source of the disturbance on a muddy field. The cobbled pathways behind the field were dyed a darker shade of stone by rain from the night before; birds sang in cubbyholes beneath guttering which adorned the nearby houses and shops; a cracked cassette lay abandoned in a bush, its tape spooled out; a rubbish bin shook as the wind blew; and a large, rather sheepish looking windmill sat squat in the middle of the field.

'Mmm,' said Whitney, stroking his chin. 'Mmm.' He paused. 'And we're sure that wasn't here before?'

Debbie nodded, then shook her head: 'Yes. No. I mean, yes, I'm sure it wasn't there before.'

'Mmm,' said Whitney. 'Mmm.'

Whitney carefully extracted a stubby yellow pencil from his pocket and a notepad, and began to scribble on it, muttering as he did so.

'Windmill... in the street... not previously there... just appeared overnight...' He paused, rolling over words in his mind. 'Very... very strange.' He nodded, and underlined the word just to make a point.

'How did it get there?' mused Debbie.

'Aha!' Whitney, said with a smile. 'Well, that's a mystery, isn't it? And that's why I'm here - to solve it.'

'You come across this sort of thing often?'

Whitney nodded: 'Yes, this sort of... strange happening is exactly what I deal with.' He smiled. 'I'll root the perpetrator out, don't you worry.'

'And what about the missing girl?' came a voice from behind.

Whitney spun around. A large crowd had gathered behind him, the sound of cameras going off and autograph pads jostling making a flurry of noise. Just for one moment, Whitney thought it was all for him. And then the owner of the voice took a step forward: a tall man with a shaven head. He wore sunglasses which had gathered raindrops, a suit so crisp and tight it looked like his natural skin, and chewed gum as he stepped forward.

'Oh!' swooned Debbie. 'It's only Timothy bloody Scottsbarn the Third!' She paused. 'Bit shorter than I'd imagined though.'

'Timothy Scottsbarn the Thir–' began Whitney, still scribbling, when he snapped out of it. 'Wait, who?'

'Who? Ha!' laughed the aforementioned Timothy. '"Who?' he asks!' He gestured to the crowd.

Whitney smiled politely, and at once the crowd burst into information.

'He's a pop star!'

'He's a detective!'

'He's a dreamboat!'

'Ladies, ladies!' laughed Timothy. 'Please, you'll make me blush!' He swung round to face Whitney. 'But they're right. Hi, I'm Timothy: pop star, adventurer, Most Fanciable Man 1985 and 1986, and amateur sleuth.' He spat out his gum. 'And quite a good one at that.' He smiled again and winked.

'He's not lying,' whispered Debbie to the increasingly confused Whitney. 'He was the one who un-masked the Masked Robber of Swansea!' She waited for a reaction from Whitney, but there was none. 'He solved the case of the Eerily Influential Teacher from Martham!' Still nothing. 'Sergeant, he can lay claim to the arrest, trial and imprisonment of the Uncatchable Brian! And he was uncatchable!'

'Sorry,' muttered Whitney. 'I'm a bit rusty on current affairs.'

'Look,' said Timothy, jabbing a finger into Whitney's stomach, 'this is a big deal and it's going to take a big deal to sort it out. You,' he said, poking him again, 'ain't it, Tubby. I am.'

'Tubby?' Whitney looked crestfallen for a moment, but then stood up straight, pulled his shoulders back and sucked in as much of his stomach as he could. Debbie took a step back as the two men squared up.

'Move on,' sneered Timothy.

Whitney did not. 'A girl went missing, you said.' He flicked through his notepad. 'When?'

'Last night,' muttered Timothy, who was holding up his fingers as if to frame the scene later on.

'And who wa—'

'Look, Tubby, shut up and let me get on with solving this.' Timothy pulled out a crumpled sheet of paper from his pocket. 'Here.'

Whitney flattened out the creases and read it. It was a police report by the looks of it, detailing the mystery of a missing student. Her name was Joanna, she was studying Politics and Economics at the University of Sussex, and she had last been seen around the same time the windmill was first sighted. There was a photo at the top of the sheet showing a slim, happy girl at a party.

'How did you get this?' pondered Whitney. 'Looks official.'

'Downing Street,' beamed Timothy. 'Oh yes, me and Mrs. Thatcher,' he snapped his fingers, 'we're like that. In fact the Prime Minister trusts me so much that she's instructed the local plods to stay out of my way until I send for them. And that means you, Tubbs.'

'Yes, well, that's very good sir, but this Mrs Thatcher isn't here right now, so I rather think I should get down and do some detective work.' Whitney pulled a magnifying glass out of one of his pockets. 'But where to start?'

Timothy looked both annoyed amused. 'You're persistent, I'll give you that. Stupid, though. What have you discovered?'

'Discovered? Well, nothing yet, sir,' smiled Whitney. 'I'll have to get on my hands and knees and find out.'

'You see?' Timothy jeered, playing to his audience again. 'Stupid!'

The crowd laughed and Whitney felt small. 'Well, sir, what have you discovered then?'

'Who, me?' smiled Timothy, innocently. 'Well, nothing much yet, but...'

Timothy jumped up and started to dart around the place, his eyes flitting to and fro and his words pouring out, tumbling one on top of the other.

'There are piled up flecks of a distinctive green nail varnish here on the grass,' began Timothy, serious now. 'There are also marks on the mud left by the heavy indentation of stationary footsteps, indicative of the victim chipping her nails whilst waiting for some time.' He ran to the rubbish bin. 'At the top of the rubbish bin there is a magazine and a book. They both have the corners of pages folded over, a rather habitual trait which suggests that the same person was reading them both and folded the pages as placeholders. And then, of course, there's the fact that both the magazine and the book are slightly mud-stained and trodden in: so, probably dropped and discarded in the ensuing struggle when the kidnapping commenced, then presumably picked up and thrown away by a dustbin man with a clubbed foot, as noted by footsteps elsewhere in the mud leading to and from said bin with one mark far heavier than the other, footsteps which continue on the pathway for a bit before being washed away by the rain.' Timothy removed his sunglasses and smiled.

Whitney noticed that his mouth was open, startled and completely, utterly and thoroughly impressed. 'Well, I'll be, sir! That was certainly brilliant!'

'I certainly am,' agreed Timothy, walking back towards a now cheering crowd.

'Wait! Sir!' called Whitney.

Slowly, sighing, Timothy turned back round. 'Yes?'

'Well, sir, brilliant though that was, there is one tiny thing you have failed to account for.'

'Which is?'

'This enormous windmill which mysteriously appeared last night without prior warning. I can understand how you may have missed it, sir, what with it being only a little bit enormous and it not being in those documents from your Mrs. Thatcher...'

'The windm–' Timothy snarled. 'Yes, yes, alright, the windmill. I've only just arrived, Tubby, I don't know every tourist attraction in this damn–' He took a deep breath and started over. 'Fine. I'll... I'll tell you later. I've got a dumb cripple to find first.' He linked arms with a couple of women and laughed, turning back only to look, slightly irked, at the windmill. 'Let's leave old Tubby here to clean up the mess,' he muttered and with that, he walked away.

'Dumb cripple?' Whitney shook with anger.

'How dare he?' growled Debbie, walking back over to Whitney. 'Guess that looks aren't everything.'

'No, indeed not,' fumed Whitney. 'Oh, he can call me names all he likes, but you do not take cheap shots at people just because they're crippled. That's just...just.... Well, it's just not on.' He shook his head, suddenly resolute. 'You may wish to return to the Balmy Badger. I will be some time.'

'Don't stay out too late,' said Debbie, 'and make sure you show him a thing or two!' And with that, she scurried off as Whitney rubbed a fingerprint off the lens of his magnifying glass and set to work.

The occasional person stopped for a moment to look at the funny little policeman on his hands and knees, apparently investigating every individual blade of grass with his magnifying glass, forever jotting down notes with his pencil and notepad and laughing to himself and writing clear descriptions of every item of rubbish within the bin and nearby, from rotting apples to discarded audio cassettes (the purpose of which he needed one of these occasional people to explain to him). They soon moved on though as Whitney dusted himself down and began to sniff around the footprints in the mud one more time, just to be sure he hadn't missed anything at all, because anything, no matter how small, could be the key to solving the mysteries of the missing girl and the windmill.

It began to rain, hard. Whitney closed his eyes tight: think of Hopper. Think of Joanna. Think of the mystery and find the solution.

He carried on searching.

He looked once again through his notepad. He had reached the exact same solution as Timothy regarding the nail varnish and literature after noticing that the magazine in fact came with a free bottle of it, bottle green, and that there were tiny dots of it upon the cover of the book. It was the mysterious windmill that was causing the real confusion. There were no signs of struggle near it, but blades of grass had been flattened into large, crushed oblongs.

One enigma after another.

Tired now, Whitney leaned against the windmill, and immediately he found himself wobbling. Steadying himself and covering his ankles in mud, Whitney took a step back and looked at the windmill again. He tentatively stepped forward and hit it. The windmill wobbled. He tapped it: it was completely hollow.

'Well, I'll be...' Whitney scratched his head. The windmill wasn't really a windmill at all, then. Musing over this, and more than a little pleased that he'd discovered this when Timothy had not, Whitney decided to call it a day. He walked away, leaving the hauntingly incongruous windmill with its arachnid sails behind him.

The rain thundered but Whitney focused on dinner instead of the fact he was soaked: the gravy, the sausages, the potatoes, the carrots, the...the awful noise coming from his beloved pub.

There was something in the water turning people into maniacs, or so it appeared when Whitney entered. Gone was the feeling of cosiness, replaced by several angry locals screaming and Debbie defiantly trying to sort it all out.

Whitney pulled out his trusty whistle.

PEEEEEEEEEEEEEEEEEEEEEEEEEEEEEEEEEEEEEEEEEEEEP!

The pub fell silent.

'Now, what's all this racket about then?' asked Whitney, getting out his notepad.

It took a good couple of hours to hear everybody out, but the story told was near identical every time: Timothy had been here, his entourage behind him. Star-struck and wanting to rub shoulders with giants, Symms had insisted on buying him champagne and the more they drank, the louder and more provocatively they talked: the world was a crazy place, with students doing nothing while Feminists, gays, foreigners and single parents demanded rights and benefits and no-one prepared to say anything about it. And then, drunk as much on his own powers of deduction as the alcohol, Timothy had pointed an unsteady finger at Hopper and said,

'And now even the cripples are at it, kidnapping young women.'

And it was then that all hell had broken loose.

Symms and Timothy had quickly scarpered, and now it was far beyond closing time and Whitney was there with David, helping Debbie to tidy up the pub.

'Should have barred them earlier,' sighed Debbie, 'but business was booming with them in and...' She shook her head. 'I made a mistake.'

'You weren't to know,' comforted Whitney. 'Where's Hopper?'

'Upstairs in the spare room. As soon as Timothy went on about cripples, the knives were out for him.' Debbie shook her head. 'I've never seen him so distressed, Whitney.'

'This is terrible!' moaned David. 'Lewes has never seen the like of it!'

'It will be fine, sir,' soothed Whitney. 'Timothy will go, I will clear Hopper's name, the girl will be found, and then you can bring the community back together with your play.'

David smiled. 'I hope so, I really hope so. Well, goodnight.'

After she was sure David was out of earshot, Debbie looked askance at Whitney. 'Did you mean that? About being able to clear Hopper's name?'

Whitney let out a deep sigh. 'I hope so Debbie. It's all circumstantial, but what evidence there is seems to point at him. But I don't believe it. I've sat down with the man, had a drink with him. I've been a police officer for more years than you've probably been alive. You learn a few things, like how to size a man up quickly, to work out what he's about.'

'Only men?' asked Debbie with a smile. 'What about women?'

Whitney muttered something indistinguishable, went as red as a Christmas bauble, and pretended to be very interesting in the weft of the nearby rug.

'So, Hopper?' said Debbie, tactfully steering the conversation back to where it had been going.

'My point is that there's no way I will believe Hopper is responsible for this unless I have absolute concrete proof. He's just not got this in him. I'll just have to keep searching until I find the evidence that proves his innocence. It has to be there, I just need to put the pieces together properly so I can see it.'

'Well, I don't envy you that. That crime scene was a mess. I tried to follow all the footprints in the mud but they all got mixed in together after a while. And I can't for the life of me see what that windmill has got to do with anything.'

'Me neither, at least not yet. But I'll get there. A good night's sleep will help with that so I'll say goodnight.'

'Goodnight Sergeant. Sweet dreams.'

However, Whitney was sure that his dreams would be anything but sweet.

The pressure of a mystery unsolved haunted Whitney throughout a sleepless night, and so when Debbie knocked on his door in the early hours once again, he was not what you would call refreshed, and he was certainly not happy when he heard the news: another student had vanished and another... strange thing had appeared.

Whitney took a few moments to re-read his notes from yesterday and brush his teeth and then he was out, walking to a children's park where the swings, slides and roundabout had been joined with an alarmingly large steam train.

'Oh, bother,' frowned Whitney, walking over to the locomotive with a feeling that his day was about to get worse.

Suddenly, there was a loud cough behind him. Whitney spun around to see Timothy who had presumably come from the other side of the train.

'She was last spotted here,' he said absently. 'The student that is, Tubby. Do keep up. Not sure why yet, but I'll work it out. And once again we find ourselves surrounded by footprints, many of which indicate a heavier tread on one foot. Our crip strikes again!'

'I thought you were going to arrest him yesterday.'

'Oh, do shut up Whitney,' Timothy spat on the ground. 'You're beginning to get annoying.'

'You mean you need more evidence, or do citizen's arrests not count? I take it you haven't been granted special powers by your Mrs. Thatcher?' An angry silence suggested he was right. 'What about the windmill, sir?'

'Flat pack, of course,' responded Timothy cooly. 'You could tell by the rectangular imprints upon the grass where it had been laid pre-assembly. I've already found the same imprints over there to save you the bother of proving your incompetence again. Now, why don't you stay here and play with the choo-choo train while I go and track down our missing cripple?' He waved. 'So long.'

Whitney watched Timothy leave, and began pacing up and down. Two girls missing, an arrogant monster showing him up, and poor Hopper being blamed. As hours went, this wasn't exactly his finest. He went back to the train and the footprints and started to take notes. He noticed a strand of ginger hair caught in the chain-link fence – the second missing student's hair, he presumed. He took the measurements of the train. He compared these new footsteps with yesterday's and decided that, yes, they did indeed belong to the same person, mixed in though they were with those of the various other people who'd traipsed over this spot in the last few days.

It was only as night fell that the obvious struck him: Hopper couldn't possibly have done anything untoward with the now missing student; he had spent the entire night in the spare room at the Balmy Badger, hiding.

'Curiouser and curiouser,' said Whitney, staring at the footprints.

When the following morning arrived with another missing girl in tow, Whitney felt cold and as though he hadn't slept for months now.

Whitney was not in the mood to tolerate any nonsense from anyone anymore, and thankfully neither was Timothy. Whitney might not have liked the amateur sleuth but he had to admit that he had a brilliant mind and right now it was focussed on solving the mystery at hand. The two of them found themselves in a back alley, strewn with litter, the harsh, tangy smell of vomit and a chest, with a cape, fake moustache and elaborate ball gown abandoned beside it.

'I think,' said Whitney, 'that it's time we called in someone else.'

'Nonsense,' crowed Symms, who had taken to following Timothy around like a stray puppy dog, hanging on his every word. 'Timothy can do it better than anyone else, can't you, Timothy?'

'Oh, shut up, Jeremy!' replied Timothy. He bent down to look at the chest. 'Just go away and leave me to it.'

'Oh...' Symms looked red-faced now, holding his large keys tight for comfort. 'Well, sure, I'll be in the pub. I'll get the round in.'

'Yes yes yes,' muttered Timothy, paying the banker no attention.

Thunder clapped in the way thunder so often does, and the detectives detected.

Whitney decided to wander the streets that night, focussing on the immediate area in which the disappearances had taken place. He had not been able to sleep properly since the first young woman had gone missing, and whenever he tried his mind filled with the clues, taunting him with his failure to correctly put them together.

Timothy had a new hypothesis: that the strange items were totems; little trinkets left behind as a calling card by the villain thanks to his egotism (definitely Hopper; he must have snuck out the night before).

Bunkum! Whitney thought. If they were calling cards, then why had the chest and its contents been left here, there and everywhere instead of neatly organized like the train and windmill had been?

His reveries were disturbed by the sound of some kind of disturbance − raised voices, scuffling sounds. Fearing the worse, Whitney ran towards the source of the noise − a grubby bottle bank, fenced off and hidden away. He blew his whistle as hard as his state of breathlessness would allow.

'Stop!' he called, switching on his torch. 'You're caught. You're–' he started to repeat, then halted.

There, in his beam, caught with dust motes and a couple of flies, was Timothy, holding Hopper, one of his arms winched up behind his back.

'So, I thought I'd walk round Lewes tonight, looking in all the places our criminal hadn't been,' sneered Timothy. 'And, lo and bloody behold Whitney, look who I found?'

'Oh, Hopper...' started Whitney, but he could go no further, knocked numb by the sense of thorough disappointment.

'It wasn't me, honest!' stuttered Hopper.

'Then why are you here?'

'I was walking back from the Badger, saw someone snooping here and went to look! It was...' started Hopper, when there was a cough and David emerged from behind the bottle bank.

'Ta-dah,' said David, stepping forward sheepishly.

'Oh, David...' sighed Whitney. This was not a good night.

'No!' said David, suddenly. 'No, I didn't kidnap anyone, I promise!'

'Then why are you here?' spat Timothy, confused now, yanking Hopper's arm again to vent his frustration.

David floundered. 'Look, it's been a bad time for the society.'

'Society?' butted in Timothy.

'The Amateur Dramatics society,' blinked David as if it was the most obvious thing in the world. 'Our audiences have been low and we've this farce to put on, and so I...' he shook his head. 'I thought I'd do some creative advertising; something to get people talking. So I got props from the play and decided I'd scatter them, to advertise the play. It's a good old-fashioned farce: trouble at the old windmill! People in frocks tied down to train tracks by wicked men with capes and moustaches, that sort of thing!'

'So the windmill... the train... the cape...' reeled off Whitney.

'All mine, yes. I was going to put a fake saw here because there's been no-one snatched tonight by the sounds of it, when these two startled me.'

'If you're so innocent,' gnashed Timothy, 'why were your 'props' at the crime scenes?'

'Well, the windmill was a co-incidence,' admitted David. 'I erected it and was going to put some posters on it the next day when everything kicked off. I put the train out and the next missing girl went to see it when she was taken. Then I got clever. Last night, I was too late: I heard a cry, went to where I'd heard it, and quickly left my props there. Great publicity, no?' He smiled, as if he'd said something incredibly clever.

Whitney gaped, horrified. 'You've taken advantage of terrible misfortune!'

'Bollocks,' snarled Timothy. 'You kidnapped the ladies, the crip here was your accomplice.'

David looked outraged. 'Why would I kidnap any ladies?'

'I don't know,' replied Timothy, shaking his head. 'Torture? Blackmail? Sex?'

'Sex?' David laughed. 'Timothy, I'm as gay as a bloody maypole.'

Timothy's mouth flapped like a goldfish, as he tried to reconcile the facts with his theory, stuttering suggestions into the night air, but Whitney wasn't listening.

Not David, then, he thought.

Of course not David, he answered himself. He's a bally fool, but nothing more. And like he said, what would be his motive? Without the windmill and train obscuring the matter, the case suddenly seemed so much clearer, a simple matter of basic detection. Who would be behind the kidnapping of young women? Someone with an interest in them? Someone with a vendetta against them?

Oh...oh....What about someone currently going through a nasty divorce? Someone who's been listening to Timothy's every word about the case and trying to stir up his prejudices as a distraction?

'Oh yes,' said Whitney, aloud. 'Oh yes, someone like that indeed.'

And then the most obvious thing hit him. The footprints in the mud...It had been staring him in the face the whole time. It had even been pointed out to him!

Whitney turned away from the scene before him and started to run.

'Hey!' shouted Timothy after him. 'Where are you going?'

'Oh, pardon me, sir,' shouted Whitney over his shoulder, adjusting his helmet and putting his whistle to his lips as he ran. 'I have a kidnapper to catch!'

'Oh no you don't!' gasped Timothy, chasing after him. 'The case is mine!'

He chased Whitney down streets, past the Balmy Badger, across roads, until they reached a large, familiar house.

'But... but this is Jeremy's house,' said Timothy, looking at it.

Whitney hammered on the front door: 'Symms! This is the police: open up!'

There came no reply, so, with a short run up, Whitney threw himself shoulder-first at the door, which flew open easily, leaving Whitney in an embarrassed heap on the floor. Dusting himself down, he ran through the house, still blowing his whistle.

No-one in the living room, the dining room, the bathroom, the kitchen, but what about the cellar?

Slowly, Whitney opened the cellar door and crept down the stairs, but he needn't have bothered. He could already hear crying.

'Hello?' said Whitney, fearful of what he would find. 'Is everybody alright down here?'

Jeremy Symms appeared at the foot of the stairs and raised his fist as if to strike him. For one moment, it looked like he would, but then he stopped instead and crumpled to the ground, crying.

Whitney swept his torch around the cellar: Symms's wife was tied to a stone pillar, blood on her forehead matching the blood on Symms's keys. He swept it further around the room and picked out the faces of three very scared and tired women bound with ropes against chairs. He instantly recognized Joanna, the first student, from her photograph.

'It's the bloody women!' cried Symms, vaguely pointing at them all and slurring his words. 'The stupid, stupid women! They treat us like bloody fools! It was... it was her fault!' He pointed to his wife. 'Wanting a divorce, wanting to take money that I'd spent years working for. ' He spat on the floor. 'That is not how it works!' There was a long, dead silence. 'She wouldn't back down. I was going to lose all I'd worked for. And these others, they're just as bad, they just haven't found someone to trick into marrying them yet. I wanted to stop this happening to other people. They're all the same. You know that, don't you?' he asked, imploringly.

But Whitney did not respond. He pushed Symms aside, realising that the pathetic creature was too broken to be a risk to anyone now. 'Hello, everyone,' he said to the frightened women. He let out a breath he hadn't realized he'd been keeping in. 'It's alright. It's over now.'

The media scrum around the house was immense; quite unlike anything Whitney had ever seen. He quickly excused himself from the crowd, watching as doctors, nurses, and policewomen and -men slowly helped the kidnapped women out of the house to great, whooping cheers of relief.

The cheers quickly died down when Symms was dragged out by the real police, kicking and screaming.

'It wasn't my fault!' he spluttered. 'It was them; the women! They're to blame! They're ruining society!'

Whitney tried to keep out of the way as Symms was escorted into the back of a police van. Timothy had disappeared, presumably not wanting to be connected in any way to a case he failed to solve, and certainly not one in which he'd been cosy with the criminal himself.

Whitney turned away. It was over now. It was over, and so was the holiday. He put his whistle away and sighed. Lewes wouldn't be the same, and neither would his presence here. There would be questions, and the answers he gave would never satisfy anyone, especially when they looked into his background and found that he didn't even exist here. That perfect place with its fires and Balmy Badgers and laughing: all gone now.

Whitney thought of David. Somehow, the fact he had done so wrong was worse than the rest of this... this mess.

'Well,' he said to no-one at all, looking at his pocket-watch. 'Time to go.'

'Hey!'

Whitney turned around: it was Hopper.

'Hey, you can't just go!'

'Well, I...'

'Nonsense! You have to stay!

'He's right, you know,' chimed in another voice: Debbie's. She ran up to Whitney, planted a kiss on his cheek and threw her arms around him. He felt himself burn crimson with embarrassment.

'What you need is a good meal, a hot bath, and a pint of whatever takes your fancy,' smiled Debbie. 'I'm going to pamper you rotten, Sergeant.'

'And I do owe you at least one!' Hopper added.

'Actually Hopper,' said Whitney, untangling himself awkwardly (and slightly reluctant) from Debbie's embrace, 'it's Debbie here that you owe.'

'Me?' Debbie replied, incredulous. 'What did I do?'

'Why, you only solved the crime.'

'I did?' Both Debbie and Hopper looked at Whitney, baffled.

'Absolutely. You were the first one to suggest that the props and kidnappings might not be connected.'

'Well, not exactly, I just said...'

'But more than that, you were the one to spot the flaw in both Timothy's and my thinking. All those footprints in the mud. Hopper's were there because he goes there because of his job, so it was easy to assume that the footprints leaving the scene that all the tracks that resembled Hopper's were actually his. After all, it was hard to follow the tracks from start to finish. But Symms had to remove his victims from the scene someone, and what would be the easiest way of doing it?'

And then Debbie understood. 'He'd carry them over one shoulder, which would push one of his feet down more heavily! That's brilliant!'

'And I only thought of it because you managed to cut through all the tangles Timothy and I were getting ourselves into. If I'd listened to you earlier there might have only been one kidnapping to investigate. Have you ever thought of a career in the police force?'

'Me? I'm not sure...'

'Oh, come now, you're a natural. At least promise me you'll think about it.'

'Ok,' said Debbie, 'I'll promise on one condition. That you spend the weekend here at the pub's expense before you go off back to your own station. I absolutely insist.'

'You do?'

'Oh yes.' Her deer-like eyes glowed as she smiled in the twilight.

Whitney looked between Debbie and Hopper, and realised with some pleasure that he really had no choice.

'Oh...go on then,' he said, and they walked arm-in-arm towards the Balmy Badger.

Mr Dogberry's Christmas
Philip Craggs

It was around two in the morning when Cassie saw the star fall.

She had been woken up by the last of her mum's guests slamming the front door behind them. Despite the bang she doubted it had woken her mother, who would probably sleep on the settee until early afternoon as usual. Cassie had so gotten used to these late-night parties that they didn't really bother her any more, even though she thought tonight's was probably louder than usual, on account of it being Christmas Eve. A thought struck her and she glanced at her little bedside clock. No, not Christmas Eve – Christmas Day.

She got out of bed and ran to the window, pulling the curtain aside. It was snowing! Not heavily, just enough for the pavement to be dusted, just enough for it to stick. And, as she looked, a star fell from the sky. Despite the snow she saw it clearly, getting bigger and brighter as it got closer to the ground until it disappeared from sight behind some buildings.

A fallen star! That meant...well...Cassie couldn't quite remember what it meant but she thought it involved wishes and other good things. And if a bad person got to it first they could do bad things with it. Was that right? She was sure she'd heard that somewhere.

She didn't know what to do for the best. Her mum didn't like her getting up once she'd been sent to bed, but then this was for a special reason. Assuming her mum believed her and didn't just think she was after attention, in which case she'd probably slap the back of her legs. But she had to do something.

Cassie slipped on her old and ill-fitting dressing gown and crept downstairs. If her mother was awake then they could maybe look for the star together. But, when she slowly pushed open the door of the living room, she found her asleep as she had expected. She took a step closer and kicked over a bottle that skidded across the floor. Her mother did not stir.

Right, thought Cassie decisively, that settles it.

She turned and went back up to her bedroom. She opened her wardrobe and looked at the few items that hung there. What do you wear to collect a fallen star? Remembering the snow she decided to wear the warmest clothes she had, her thick pink coat and wellington boots. And she would take her school back-pack to carry the star in when she found it.

She was ready to go. There was just one thing left to consider. She knew she was not supposed to go out at night – her teachers had told her so. It was dangerous for little girls to be out alone at night, even if they were looking for fallen stars. There was no way that her mother would come out with her, even if she could wake her up. So there was only one option left, someone who never let her down and would protect her, whatever happened.

'Come on Big Bear,' she said, picking the two foot toy from her bed. 'Let's go and find the star.'

It was colder outside than Cassie could remember it ever being. She hugged Big Bear close and walked towards the area where she saw the star fall. The streets were empty but she could hear music and voices from houses in which the Christmas parties were still going on. She moved as quickly as she could, not wanting to encounter any strangers.

She walked for about ten minutes until she realised that she did not know exactly where the star had fallen. She had walked just out of the residential area towards the high street with its charity shops and boarded up windows. But now she did not know where to go next.

'Oh Big Bear,' she asked her companion, 'what shall we do?' Big Bear looked at her impassively. 'You're right,' she said with a nod. 'We'll go a little bit further, then go home.'

She passed a few more shops and was about to give up when she noticed that the alleyway to her right was lighter than it should have been. She made her way into the alley, heading towards the light which got brighter and brighter until her eyes started to hurt. She held Big Bear in front of her face (his back to the light so he wouldn't hurt his eyes either) and shuffled until she guessed she was stood right in front of it. There was a cardboard box on the floor by her feet. She knelt down, picked up the box and threw it down. The light instantly dimmed and she lowered Big Bear and looked in front of her. The box she had thrown down was glowing with an unearthly light.

'We found it Big Bear!' she said, holding him up in celebration, 'We found it!'

But what to do now? If she couldn't even look at it she couldn't pick it up to move it. But she couldn't just leave it either. And then she had an idea.

'Listen Big Bear, we can't move this by ourselves. But I saw a police station just down the road. So, I'm going to get a policeman to come and help. But I need you to stay and make sure no-one steals the star while I'm gone. You're going to have to be very brave and scare off anyone who comes for it. Can you do that?'

Big Bear just looked at her.

'Sorry Big Bear, of course you can. Now, give me a big cuddle and I'll be back as quickly as I can.'

She sat Big Bear carefully down in front of the glowing box and walked back to the street. As she stepped back onto the pavement she glanced back and saw Big Bear in silhouette, ready for anything that came along. She hurried away into the night, wishing she was as brave as him because she felt really scared on her own.

It wasn't that Dogberry didn't like Christmas.

'Come on Dogberry,' said Clarissa. 'Come out with us. Let's see what this century has to offer.'

'That's very kind of you my dear,' said the old man, 'but I think I'll let you younger people have your fun. After our recent adventure I rather feel I could do with getting some sleep.'

Whitney and Wilson exchanged glances, and Dogberry knew they were reflecting on the group's recent close call involving genetically engineered monsters prowling the streets of twenty-first century Manchester. Even the normally unflappable Dogberry had had to admit that they had come close to being a four-course monster meal, and he suspected that it was the very closeness of the shave that had made the others so determined to stay in this unpleasant century to celebrate Christmas. Dogberry however wanted nothing more than some peace and quiet to pursue his experiments in, and saw his colleague's desire to involve him in their celebrations as nothing but a distraction. It was, he reflected, time to play the age card. In fact Dogberry was far from exhausted, but this was one of those occasions when his elderly appearance caused others to underestimate his abilities, and he was not against playing up to the prejudices of the young if it meant getting his way. With that in mind, he lent more heavily on his walking stick, as though requiring its support.

'Come along Miss,' said Wilson. 'I think Mr Dogberry could do with his sleep, especially after the last few days.'

Clarissa reluctantly conceded, and they headed out into the snowy night to find themselves some fun. The door closed heavily behind them, and Dogberry let out a sigh of relief. He knew that the others thought him something of a killjoy but it wasn't that at all. It was just that he had seen so many Christmas' that it had become a bit like a birthday to him – a day like any other to be spent most likely in his own company, or to be not noticed in the middle of an experiment or quest. And, in truth, if he'd been asked for the perfect way to spend a Christmas Day, he would have chosen to spend the hours alone with his test-tubes and gaudily-coloured chemical mixtures.

Having poured himself a generous helping of Darjeeling in the back office, he returned to the waiting room to collect the chemical formulas that he needed for tonight's experiments from his jacket pocket. He stepped out from behind the counter and stopped dead. Stood in the middle of the room was a child. He peered at it. Female, maybe nine or ten years old? Dogberry could not be sure – he found children generally baffling and had spent little time contemplating them so always struggled to guess their ages.

'Er...hello?'

'Hello,' said the child. 'Are you a policeman? You look too old to be a policeman.'

'Well...not exactly. I mean...'

'Then what are you doing in a police station?' she asked.

'Well my dear, are you a policeman?'

'Of course I'm not. I'm a *girl*. Girls aren't policemen, silly.'

'Then what are you doing in a police station?'

'*Looking* for a policeman,' she replied, with the gravity of someone who knew they were giving an absolutely sensible answer to someone who was talking nonsense but should be humoured.

It was then that Dogberry noticed that she was shaking and remembered that outside it was late at night and snowing.

'Good grief child,' he said, springing into action. He handed her his cup of tea and advised her to sip it slowly, before fetching one of Clarissa's short jackets to put around the child's shoulders.

'Now then,' he said when finished, 'what in heaven's name brings you out alone in the middle of a night like this?'

'Well,' she said with a serious nod, clearly trying to get her story into an order that this strange old man could understand. 'I was looking for a star.'

'A star? But you would surely be able to see them as clearly from your bedroom window?'

The child sighed. 'Not a *normal* star, silly. The one that fell out of the sky.'

'Out of the sky?' Dogberry leaned forwards on his stick, his features no longer a mask of confusion but of rapt concentration. 'Did you actually see it fall?'

'Well *of course* I did, or else I wouldn't have come out looking for it, would I?'

'Did you see where it landed?'

'Oh yes. We found it, but couldn't move it so I came to get help. My name's Cassie by the way. What's yours?'

'What? Oh. Dogberry, my dear. Mr Dogberry.'

'Only a Mr? So you're not a policeman then?' She looked downhearted at the realisation.

'Well no, I'm not a policeman exactly. But I help them on their cases and I am very interested in this star you've found. Now, you said 'we' when you said you found it,' he said as he shrugged himself into his thick overcoat.

'I've left Big Bear guarding it. He'll be fine but I don't want him to have to stay out too long. He doesn't like the cold, even though he's a polar bear. He's gotten used to sleeping in a bed and has gone a little bit soft because of it. But don't tell him I said that. Come on. We need to hurry or someone bad might get the three wishes.'

And with that, she grabbed his hand and led him from the station into the dark streets.

Cassie knew she should go slower, that old people take more time to do everything. But (and she didn't admit this fully, even to herself) she was worried about Big Bear. She knew that he fought Monsters every night and kept her safe, but they were Bedroom Monsters. What if Outside Monsters were different? What if more than one attacked at once? Of course, she couldn't tell Mr Dogberry that was the reason – Big Bear would be very upset if he thought she'd doubted him. So instead she complained of the cold, and how the quicker they got there, the quicker they could get back into the warmth of the police station.

She led him through the quiet streets, and then turned into the alleyway in which she had found the star. And there, to her delight and relief, was the reliable figure of Big Bear, sat in front of the glowing cardboard box.

'Oh Big Bear!' she cried. 'You're so good. Look, Mr Dogberry, I told you it would be safe with Big Bear guarding it.' She scooped Big Bear into her arms and gave him a delighted squeeze before turning him around until he faced Dogberry. 'Big Bear, I want you to meet Mr Dogberry. Mr Dogberry's a sort-of policeman, and he's going to help us look after the star. Say hello, Big Bear.' She held Big Bear's paw out towards Dogberry. Big Bear was a rather scruffy, stained white. One leg had a clear tear at the seam and he bore all the signs of a bear so treasured that Dogberry felt certain that it was the only one the girl had ever had – and had probably been bought second hand.

Dogberry reached out his hand and took the bear's paw as solemnly as if he were meeting the Prime Minister. 'Pleased to meet you, Big Bear,' he said, giving the paw a firm shake.

'Big Bear is really brave,' said Cassie. 'Every night when I go to sleep he stays awake and guards me. And if any Monsters come to get me he fights them off. Sometimes he doesn't even have to fight – they look at him and get scared and run away.'

'I'm not surprised!' said Dogberry with a chuckle, slightly surprised at the ease with which he was managing to converse with this strange creature.

'But sometimes a Big Monster comes and Big Bear gets a scratch. That's how he got the hole at the top of his leg.'

'Oh dear. Can't your mother fix it for him?'

Cassie looked at the ground. 'Mummy doesn't fix things.'

Dogberry realised he should change the subject. 'Now, let's look at this star he's been guarding, eh?'

He reached out and slowly lifted the box. As soon as he raised it even a millimetre, an intense light shot out through the gap. As the light hit his shoes he felt his toes tingle. Slowly, he raised the box higher, hoping his eyes would grow accustomed to the light in stages. Finally, with the command to Cassie that she cover her face with Big Bear's body, he threw the box completely to one side, peering at the star through his fingers. Even then, the light was too bright, so he reached into a pocket and produced a pair of sunglasses. With them on he could just about bare to look at the star for a couple of seconds, before hastily dropping the box back over it and removing the glasses.

'I feel all weird when the light comes out,' said Cassie.

So did Dogberry. Whatever the object was, he had never seen the like. It was almost impossible to tell its shape for certain because the light seemed to come off it in tendrils, but it appeared to be roughly football-sized and equally spherical. It had clearly crashed down, based on the damage to the concrete around it. A fallen star indeed...

His attention was brought back to the moment in hand by a startled scream from Cassie. He turned, and immediately saw what had terrified her. It was hard to take it in – his vision recoiled from its horrific form. He could tell that it stood around eight foot tall on tree trunk legs. Its skin was leathery with tiny patches of hair dotted over its torso. Its arms were strangely skinny, with skeletal fingers that flexed with the excitement of the prospective kill. It was one of the creatures that had nearly put paid to the lives of all four of the time travellers after their arrival, one that must have slipped away in the confusion and was now being drawn to the star. And there was no doubt, as it stepped towards them with drool dripping down from its slobbering mouth, that it meant to kill them.

'What is it Mr Dogberry?' she cried.

'That, my dear,' he replied, trying to keep his voice steady, 'is a Monster.'

The Monster walked slowly towards them, but Dogberry knew that it was capable of great speed and was just toying with them, knowing they had no-where to run to. It raised both hands and stretched out its fingers, making sure they could see its dagger-like claws.

'Big Bear!' cried Cassie. 'It's a Monster. You've got to fight him!' She held him out, facing the Monster.

But Big Bear remained inert.

'Please Big Bear. You can't let the Monster get me. *Please.*'

When he again failed to spring into action she wrapped her arms around him, held him tightly to her chest and began to sob into his shoulder.

And Dogberry, feeling as helpless as Cassie and her toy, did the only thing he could possibly do. He stepped, slowly and deliberately, in front of the child, putting his frail body between her and the slavering beast that was surely about to kill them both. He had no plan, no idea of what he could do except to stand in that spot and hope he could think of something in the handful of seconds he had left of his long life. It had taken the whole team and a large slice of luck to defeat these creatures. Alone, he knew he had no chance.

And then he heard a growl *behind* him.

At first he thought that another Monster had somehow gotten into the alley by another route. He risked a glance back.

Dogberry had seen a lot in his life – things that the average person of any age would mock as ridiculous or run screaming from in terror. But even he was unprepared for what he saw next.

Big Bear was looking up at the Monster. For a moment he thought it was just the way Cassie was holding him, until he realised that Big Bear's previously plastic black eyes were now real, and that his mouth, which had been just a series of stitches across his face, was now open, revealing a set of viciously sharp-looking teeth. Cassie had been startled by the growl and took a step back, breaking the embrace.

Big Bear did not collapse to the ground. Instead he stood firmly on his two lower paws. And then he started to grow. Within seconds Big Bear was transformed into a fully grown polar bear. A fully grown, *angry* polar bear.

Dogberry put his arm around Cassie and led her behind a dustbin.

The Monster had clearly not been expecting to meet any kind of worthy opponent when it had seen the small figures in the alleyway. It stopped still, sizing up the threat of its new adversary. And then, as though at some signal only they could hear, the Monster wailed a strange battle-cry at the same moment that Big Bear threw his head back and emitted a fearsome roar. And then they attacked.

Dogberry had kept his hand firmly over Cassie's eyes and his arms over her ears during the conflict. He had forced himself to watch as the two creatures tore into each other, hoping to spy a moment in which he and Cassie could slip away. Cassie struggled in his grasp, half wanting to see and half not, desperate to know if Big Bear was ok but not prepared to deal with the idea that he might not be. Cries of pain carried from both creatures as the fight progressed and both managed to inflict injuries on the other. Dogberry rather feared the worst – the Monster had been designed as a killer, while their protector had strength and determination but seemed over-bulky and lacking in sharpness of attack. The Monster quickly took the upper hand, slashing at its opponent with lethally sharp claws, and while even when injured Big Bear – as Dogberry couldn't help but think of him – fought back with desperate ferocity, the fight appeared to be over. Big Bear's white fur was now mostly stained red, his right back leg had been so badly injured that it was all but useless, and his growls now sounded more like howls of desperation and pain than aggression. He tried to get up to mount one more attack but collapsed back to the ground. Realising that it was one blow from victory, the Monster released another of its cries, this time in triumph, and leant over the prostate figure of its enemy, ready to deliver the final blow.

A fatal mistake.

When the Monster bent forward, it lowered its neck to within Big Bear's reach. With one last effort and a howl of pain he launched himself upwards and grabbed the Monster's neck in his strong jaw. It was over in a surprisingly short time – the Monster's neck ripped as Big Bear's teeth embedded themselves and he pulled his head back. The Monster staggered backward, barely having time to realise what had happened before it collapsed to the floor.

Once sure it was safe Dogberry emerged from his hiding place, warning Cassie not to follow him. He crossed to the prostate Big Bear. Although no expert in polar bears – let alone those who had only recently been toys – Dogberry could tell he had only moments to live.

'Big Bear!'

Cassie had been unable to resist finding out what had happened to her beloved friend, and had come out from her hiding place. The sight of him badly wounded was too much for her and she pressed the side of her face against his, sobbing uncontrollably.

'Oh Big Bear! Please don't die. Who'll look after me if you're not here? What'll happen when another Monster comes, or when I need a cuddle?'

And then Dogberry realised what had to be done.

'Cassie my dear, come to me. Come on now. I think I might have an idea of how we can help Big Bear.'

Cassie looked up at him, her eyes red and streaming. 'You mean it?'

'Would I lie to you? I'm sure this will work, but you need to be stood out of the way.'

After a moment's pause, Cassie reluctantly let go of Big Bear's face. As she stepped away Dogberry could see that he was still alive, his eye following her movement.

'Now, I need you close your eyes and cover them with your hands and to wish very, very hard for Big Bear to be alright, and just like he was before, and keep wishing it until I say to stop. Can you do that?'

Cassie nodded.

'Good. Now, begin!'

Cassie closed her eyes and began to mutter under her breath. 'Please let Big Bear be alright, please let Big Bear be alright...'

Dogberry slipped his sunglasses back on before reaching out and pulling the cardboard box off the fallen star. The light from the star swelled outwards, so intense that everything went white. After leaving it as long as he could stand Dogberry threw the box back over the star. It took several moments for his eyes to recover from the shock, even with the glasses, but as his vision cleared he saw that his hunch had been correct.

'There you are Cassie. You can look now.'

Cassie took her hands away from her eyes and looked at where the dying body of Big Bear had lain...and saw Big Bear has he had been before; two feet tall, black eyes, stitched mouth. No, not quite as he had been before. His previously dirty fur practically shone and his plastic eyes seemed to almost glow. The seam at the top of his leg looked as though it had never been torn. And there was a slightly quizzical expression on his face - as well there might be, Dogberry reflected. Cassie ran across to him and took him in her arms.

'Oh Big Bear, you're all better! You were so brave. Wasn't he brave Mr Dogberry? I told you he was brave. And he looks like new. He's all...handsome. Isn't he handsome Mr Dogberry?'

Dogberry chuckled. 'Yes my dear, he's easily the most handsome and brave bear of them all.'

Cassie suddenly looked worried. 'Mr Dogberry? Will Big Bear ever do that again? Get big I mean.'

'Why, of course he will child. Every night when you're asleep and a monster comes. The same as he always has done. But I doubt you'll ever see him – because you'll always be asleep at this time of night in the future. And it's this time that the Monsters come.'

'Do monsters try to get you too Mr Dogberry?'

'It has been known,' he replied with a smile.

'Do you have a Big Bear to protect you then?'

'No my dear, I don't. But I have some friends who, in their own ways, are almost as good. Now, let's see about this star shall we?'

As if on cue, the star flared so bright that the cardboard box disintegrated. When the light hit them Dogberry felt an overpowering sense of energy and vitality, as though anything were possible if he only wanted it enough. But he had worked out the rules to this little game, and realised that he wasn't the one playing. They turned their heads away quickly before feeling a rush of air as the star shot itself back up into the sky. Dogberry stared up after it for a moment, before turning back to Cassie.

'Oh no,' she cried. 'That was my star! I wanted my wishes.'

'Wishes indeed, Cassie. I think you'll find that you've had enough wishes come true for one evening. Now, we need to get you home to your mother.'

'She won't care. She'll be asleep for ages yet.'

'Actually,' he said, smiling and resting a hand on her shoulder, 'I think you might be in for a surprise.'

It had been, by any standard, a night of the unexpected. But nothing that had occurred so far that evening was quite as surprising to Cassie as what happened when she arrived home.

Dogberry rapped firmly on the front door. Cassie was about to tell him that he didn't need to do that because she'd left it unlocked and her mother would still be asleep when the door was thrown open, revealing her mother. Cassie had a moment to register that she looked not only surprisingly sober but also wore an expression she couldn't remember seeing on her mother's face before – she looked worried, if not outright scared. She did not have long to reflect on this however, as her mother knelt down, grabbed Cassie by the shoulders and pulled her into a suffocating embrace.

'Cassie love, where have you been? I was frantic.'

And then she realised that her mother was crying.

'Don't you *ever* do something so stupid again. I've been sat here terrified while all the neighbours have been out looking for you. Anything could have happened to you. You could have been kidnapped, I might never have seen you again. What did you think you were doing?'

Cassie looked at her mother, unable to quite believe that this was the same woman that she had last seen fast asleep only a short time before. What had happened to her?

'Well,' she said, trying to get the night's events into the right order, 'first there was the star that fell out of the sky, and then I met Mr Dogberry at the police station…'

'Ahem,' Dogberry interjected. 'What the ah…delightful child is trying to say is that she went out to play in the snow, and got herself a little lost. So she did the sensible thing and came into the police station and I walked her home. I must admit that to pass the time I told her a little story about falling stars and other such nonsense, which she seems rather taken with.'

'Well, I'm so grateful to you for bringing Cassie home safely.' She looked up at Dogberry properly for the first time. 'Er...I don't mean to be rude but aren't you a little old to be a policeman?'

Dogberry sighed, but could not really object as he had played the age card himself earlier that evening.

'Never mind, all that matters is that you've brought her back. Now, I need to go and fetch her a blanket. Just a minute.'

As soon as her mother had left the room Cassie turned to Dogberry. 'What's happened to my Mum?'

Dogberry smiled and put his hand on Cassie's shoulder. 'You mean you don't know? You were the one who mentioned three wishes. I think things will be rather different for you from now on. And I really must be on my way. I have friends who will worry about me if I'm not at the station when they return. Good-night Cassie.' He reached out and scratched Big Bear between the ears. 'And good-night to you too Big Bear, and thank-you.' Dogberry was about to turn away but paused. Was it his imagination, or had Big Bear turned his head slightly to look up at him?

As Dogberry reached the door Cassie shouted after him. 'Merry Christmas Mr Dogberry!'

'What? Oh...yes. Merry Christmas Cassie. A Merry Christmas indeed!'

Auld Lang Syne
Matt Kimpton

1st January, 1887

It was, Wilson considered, the sort of day Manleigh Halt had been made for. Freezing of course, but cut through with that crisp, impossible sunlight you were always so surprised to see at the turn of the year. The air as cold as steel, but the sky so wild and blue it made you want to kiss it.

He'd grown up in this sunlight, in this town. Not yet, admittedly; his parents wouldn't move here for a good few years yet, and of course he'd not be born himself for six more months. Which was, Wilson considered, an odd sort of thought to have. But still, what's a year? Time barely creeps along in the home counties, and this was the home of his boyhood, to the last detail.

The bright, zig-zag high street with the Three Ravens on the corner. John Clanney's cart clip-clopping past the cobblers, his sons alive and well and pushing each other tumbling off the back. Even the Farriers was still a farrier's this far back: the cold air warmed by the pounding rhythm of the anvil; the surging glitter-glimmer-darkness of its sparks. It was like the lifeblood of his childhood, that sound: the very heartbeat of his memories. And yet here he was in it, alive, full-grown, doing the job he'd dreamt of all those days.

Well, nearly.

He glanced at the scrap of paper in his palm, written in Miss Miller's clean, curling hand. BUNS, she exhorted. TEA, she exclaimed (adding Typhoo Tipps in an intimate parenthesis). SUNDRIES, she whispered breathily, too fine a lady to spell out unpleasant details.

Wilson must have run the same errand, what, every day almost, when he was a lad. He swung into Finn's, the old grocer's where he'd spent those awkward mornings avoiding its mortifyingly buxom owner's eye, bracing himself for the smell of the place, the original black drawers staring down at him once more. And there, behind the counter, resplendent in her old-fashioned ruffles—

No. Not Mrs. Finn.

A woman he'd never set eyes on before. Mousy, curling hair tucked half out of sight like a scolded child. Pursed lips threatening to erupt into a scowl. A face he fought not to notice, and very nearly managed it, because it looked so plain – until he realised he couldn't look away. Because, oh lord, those eyes, so wild and blue they made him want to...

'Can I help you?'

Wilson stared at her, despite the nagging voice in his head reminding him to stop. 'Buns,' he whispered, which was probably appropriate.

'You want the bakers, two doors down,' she said, and returned to her ledger, the light of her eyes wasted on a list of grocery orders.

Now, just a moment. This was his town, his birthright. And alright, he'd never done more than gaze moon-eyed at Mrs. Finn, and in hindsight no more's the pity, but he was a man of the world now. And, by golly, if there was one thing Constable Wilson knew it was how to impress a lady.

'As a matter of fact,' he said, pulling himself sharply upright, 'I'm an officer of the law. Constable Wilson, Manleigh Halt Constabulary. And if you don't very much mind: I'd like some tea. Miss, er...'

'Kirkwell. Gladys Kirkwell. And you can look at my face if you're going to look at me at all, thank you very much Mister Constable.'

She turned smartly without waiting for a reply, and started up the store's precarious stepladder, leaving Wilson to crowbar his eyes politely down towards its lower rungs. Funny thing. Never used to have a bottom rung, that ladder: it was one of Mrs. Finn's daily reasons to curse Mr. Finn. And yet there it was, hale and hearty. Time-travel, eh?

'A pound do you?' came a voice from above.

'Er, if you would. Typhoo if you've got it.'

There was a silence the length of a small frown. 'Tea, you said.'

'Course I did, silly old me. Tea'll do nicely.'

She clambered back down, one hand clutching the paper packet – and, as her foot came into Wilson's vision, lowering itself onto the bottom step, the ladder creaked. The fateful rung, bending.

Wilson had been trained for moments like these. Time, essence, all that. Not a second wasted, he surged forward, leapt the counter in one movement, scattering eggs and jam-jars everywhere – thudded to the floor the other side – swung his arms up as the rung snapped –

And Gladys Kirkwell slipped six inches downwards, into his arms.

Her scowl, when she extricated herself, could have boiled a child. But then that was very often the case, Wilson had found, when a lady was secretly impressed. 'After all,' he reassured her, from that forbidden, private side of the counter, with what he hoped was a flashy smile, 'Everything happens for a reason.'

Miss Miller sighed. That door could really do with a lock, she thought. They couldn't seem to sit still five minutes before vagrants, ne'er-do-wells and – well, she wouldn't want to use the word 'undesirables', but everyone would start congregating. And as for this child who had wandered in, nine years old at the very most, covered in nasal excreta and wailing for a policeman...

Well, it was all very well helping the community, but really.

'Missing?' asked Sergeant Whitney, as ever trying to get to the root of the problem by licking a pencil and hoping. The boy looked at him with wide, brown eyes.

'Yes,' he said. Quavering lips, dribbling nose, it really was too much. 'He was there last night, and now... Now...'

And, there he went. Back into snivelling.

Clarissa shot a look over at Mister Dogberry, but he was pottering about at the back of the station with a broom, useless to anybody. She sighed, giving the child a stiff look.

'This is your grandfather that we're talking about?' she asked, brisk as she could manage (which turned out to be really quite brisk). The child nodded, soppy-eyed. 'And your parents, they aren't out looking for him? They didn't think to come to the police themselves?' He just stared at her.

She despaired, she really did. Tea and buns, that's all they'd come for! Still, there was no point in denying it, despite the unbearable levels of mucus involved: this was indubitably a mystery, and very likely a crime. She nodded to Whitney, poised with his pencil and notebook, waiting for the world to form an orderly queue.

'Better take down some particulars, Sergeant,' she sighed. And in they rolled. Name: Frank Draycott. Age: nine (hah!). Date of birth: June, 1913. Place of residence—

'Wait,' she snapped. Something wasn't...

's'Manleigh Halt.'

'No, wait!' It had hit her. Clarissa raced to the door, flung it open with a jangle of the bell, and stood, appalled, in the doorway.

The carriages trundling up and down. The tumble of laughter from the Farriers. The distant rattle of a motorcar heading to the manor. Unmistakeably, the sights and sounds of Manleigh Halt. Of home.

Of 1922.

1st January, 1887

They'd gone. The buggers had gone.

Wilson raced past the pub again, on his third lap of the village. Hopeless now: there was nowhere for it to be. Cap Lane hadn't even been built yet. And where the police station would stand in thirty years – where it had stood, ten minutes before – was just broad green meadows, spreading out to the hills.

I remember when this was all fields, his father's voice, self-mocking, floated round in his head. The endless clanging of the farrier's hammer pounded with him as he ran – that old, dead sound, from a place burnt down so many years ago – and with it, that old, familiar feeling of growing up: of the whole world a zig-zag high street, with Bill Rudney's on one side, and Tam Hackart on the other, and him in between, and no way out...

The bell jangled over the door as he hurtled into the grocer's: the last place anything had felt remotely normal. Miss Kirkwell raised an eyebrow at him as he leant against the door, panting: a friendly, or at least mercifully unfamiliar face.

'Are you alright, Constable? Shall I call you an actual policeman?'

Wilson gasped for breath, desperate for some hope of sanctuary. 'I was — my home... It's not... There's nowhere to... '

She frowned. Behind her, mocking advertisements for Sunlight Soap and Scott's Emulsion looked down on him, demanding to know how he thought he could possibly begin to explain.

Miss Kirkwell shook her head slowly, tutting. 'Well, now. This is what happens when you set yourself up with a lie, isn't it? Manleigh Halt Constabulary, indeed.' She looked at him for a moment, and her scowl seemed to snag on the corners of a smile as she reached for her coat. 'Come on, let me have a word with Clive at the Ravens. You saved me from a ferocious ladder. Least we can do is find you a place to stay.'

1st January, 1922

'Well, it must work. Try it with the tea-caddy open.'

'I'm afraid it already is, Miss Miller.'

'Then try it with it closed!'

The station was in what could only be described as an uproar. Sergeant Whitney had spent the last half an hour alternately pulling open and slamming the front door, with Mr. Dogberry gamely dragging furniture about, and young Master Draycott noisily being of no help whatsoever, which Clarissa understood was what one expected from a nine year old boy. She, meanwhile, was doing her best to run through every possible position of the desk drawers, and had developed what might yet prove to be a radical new species of headache.

This was the problem, Clarissa thought – and then, hastily correcting herself, thought: one of the problems – with travelling in an apparently magical police station. When it came down to it, none of them had the faintest idea how to make the thing go. Often simply closing the door was enough, which could be a pain in cold weather; Sergeant Whitney had taken to hanging a bath-towel over the top-rail to prevent them hurtling off into the ether every time they came in for a sit down. But now, just when they truly needed to return to the 1880s, and with no clue as to what had gone wrong: nothing. For all anyone could see it was a perfectly ordinary police station, albeit one containing rather a lot of rattling furniture, a certain amount of improper language, and a woman getting irrationally cross at a door.

She closed the final drawer, waited for the slam from the other side of the room, and sighed. 'Very well Mr. Dogberry, let's move the lampstand over to the northern wall if you please, and we'll start again.'

Sergeant Whitney looked at her, alarmed. 'I wouldn't know, I don't get invites to manors and suchlike, Miss.'

Ah yes, that was the other thing: the sergeant had gone mad. 'I never mentioned any such places, Sergeant Whitney.'

'What places?'

Yes, that was more or less how it went. Confinement to a secure institution would be a kindness really. Particularly, given the pounding in her head, if he could arrange to take the dratted boy with him.

On cue, Frank kicked the side of the duty desk at the zenith of his latest bout of self-pity. 'Why are you doing this? Granddad's missing, and all you can do is go on about a stupid calendar!'

That wasn't quite fair, Clarissa thought. They often used the day-calendar as a sort of ready-reckoner to gauge how fast they were 'travelling through time' (the phrase still made her feel a bit silly), so, yes, they had hoped it might shed light on how they'd swapped decades without noticing. But she'd hardly say they'd been obsessing about it. Frankly, with poor Constable Wilson stranded in the last century, they had other concerns. She gave the boy a sour look.

'Please be quiet, young man. This is a matter of serious scientific inquiry, and while you're at it could you re-open the tea-caddy for me? Thank you.'

'That's the trouble, Mr. Dogberry sir, I don't know a great deal about railways.'

'Thank you Sergeant Whitney, that will do.'

'Look, it's only a blooming calendar!'

'That's enough, young man.'

'But you're right, it is getting quieter.' Oh, sweet merciful heavens...

'Mr. Dogberry, please, not you as well! I didn't say it was getting quieter,' Clarissa snapped.

'Is it?' Sergeant Whitney looked over from the door. 'You're right.'

Clarissa frowned. 'Actually... I suppose it is a little less loud.' More than that, in fact. Without the din in the station, it was almost silent — the motorcars having passed on, and the tavern chatter shrunk to nothing. There weren't even any footsteps passing on the street.

She shook her head. 'It's like the sergeant was saying: must be an open house at the manor. Now, if we are to stand any chance of rescuing the poor constable—'

'I ain't much good at jigsaw puzzles, mind,' Frank murmured from the corner.

'Please Master Draycott, this isn't the time.'

'...But that bit fits, don't it?'

'Ahhh,' said Mr. Dogberry: a long, slow sound. 'You know, I rather think it does.'

'What are you talking about, please?'

Frank sniffed. 'You said it's open house at the manor, and just now he said he don't know 'cos he ain't never been there. Makes sense.'

Clarissa stared at him. Secure institution, the only way. Although... it did make sense, if one ignored the parts where it didn't. And, now she thought about it, she had said it was getting quieter, just after Mr. Dogberry had told her she was right about it getting quieter...

'Yes, but — but it didn't happen like that, did it? It was the other way around.'

'As I said,' said Mr. Dogberry, who hadn't yet, but then Clarissa supposed that was rather the point, 'It's a matter of causality. The whole thing is unravelling, do you see? The very fabric of cause and effect fraying at the seams.

'Oh, come now. Why ever would that happen?'

'Why indeed. Why anything, now. Everything happens for a reason, after all – but not, it would now appear, in that order. Which makes for a fourth little mystery to solve.'

Sergeant Whitney looked up from his notebook, momentarily back in the flow of the conversation. 'A fourth, Mr. Dogberry?' asked

'Yes, yes of course. We already have three, don't we? Why the station moved from one year to another without our interference. What has happened to young Frank's missing grandfather. And finally, Miss Miller... why it is so quiet, outside a public house, on New Year's Day.'

Clarissa felt the first seeds of a terrible fear growing inside her.

'I didn't say anything about a calendar,' said Sergeant Whitney, mystified.

7th April, 1890

Funny how life treated you. All that time arguing, all those prickly afternoons looking for police stations – and now suddenly, unlooked for, they had friends. Almost more than would fit into the church. Where had they all come from, eh? When had he had time for that, between the lies?

There was still the future to think about, of course. Honeymoon on the Isle of Wight, if you please. Little flat above the shop. And then, what, a move, somewhere north, there were always jobs going in the North, and he was good with his hands, at least. Just get out of Manleigh, before his past caught up with him...

But he couldn't think about any of that. Because she was there, and she was wearing white, and there was honeysuckle.

The vicar was talking. The air was full of blossom, somehow. And her eyes were so wild and blue they made him want to kiss her.

So he kissed her. It seemed the right thing to do.

1st January, 1922

There was no-one left alive in Manleigh Halt.

Clarissa had hunted high and low, in the gathering gloom of the low winter sun, but there were only shadows left to taunt her. Not one man in the streets, or in the yards. The manor looming dark and silent on the hill.

The door of the Farrier's Arms was open, welcoming as ever, but when she poked her head gingerly inside, there was nothing left but the stale smell of drink. Half-finished pints of what she assumed was ale stood on tables, a scattering of skittles still standing in their hood by the bar. It was like a still-life, robbed of the very lives that made it worthwhile.

None of them spoke as they wandered from door to door. It seemed almost sacrificial to break the silence. Sergeant Whitney just frowned into his notebook, scribbling some indecipherable diagram – a stubborn, angry scribble at what his home had become. Mr. Dogberry was down on his knees, a jeweller's loupe in his eye and a magnifying glass in hand, studying walls, pavements, the stones of the street. The boy just wandered, wide-eyed, alone.

After a while she'd grown bolder, and started pushing her face up against windows, listening at doors. The house a few doors down from them, the Marriners' she thought it was, lovely family, had supper on the table. She could make out knives and forks dropped on the plates, among the half-eaten vegetables. There was a fork on the chair nearest the window, a gobbet of mashed potato still clinging to the tines.

Not a dog barking. Not a child crying. No-one.

'You've noticed the plants?' Dogberry asked eventually, as they passed each other outside the dark door of the old grocer's, this morning a funeral parlour, now a crypt.

She hadn't, of course. You always miss what's right in front of you – or in this case, what isn't. The village green was brown, when she stared hard enough to see it: not a blade of grass to be seen. It wasn't just the sheep that were missing from the dark hills; the hills themselves had lost their lustre. Even the towering oak that used to stand outside the Shade, the tree that gave the pharmacy its name, was gone: just a deep, root-drilled hole in the empty ground.

'Not with a bang,' murmured Mr. Dogberry behind her, 'But a whimper.'

He was standing by what had once been the cricket pitch, now just a blacker strip in the dark earth, a handful of dirt in his crabbed, gloved hands. He offered it to her, as if in explanation. She stared at him, as if to ask for a rather better one. He sighed.

'Nothing,' he said. 'Not even the most microscopic lifeform, smaller than a hundredth of an inch, is left. We were safe in the station, of course, but beyond that... It's the end. The end of all life in the world.'

She stared at him, dumbstruck. Death, on such a scale – it was absurd. Hours ago the village had been ringing with life. And yet, the silence, the darkness...
'But how?' she whispered. 'What could possibly have caused such devastation?'

Mr. Dogberry removed the loupe from his eye, and looked at her with a careful, calm expression.

'I'm afraid there's only one possible explanation, Miss Miller. We know that life ought to continue. We have seen the future. And for those with the power to change the past, we have only one name.'

His eyes glistened in the darkness. And he said, sadly: 'Us.'

* * *

25th November 1891

Dawn was just coming up. They'd have the whole town awake if they weren't careful. But who cared, right now? Let 'em hear her. They'd waited so long — those sad false hopes, lying in the arms of strangers in the ground. The deafening clamour of friends not saying anything. But not today.

She had his nose, poor mite. But then she had her mother's cheeks to make up for it, and those wild blue eyes, and a pair of lungs on her, that much was clear.

One day he'd have to tell her about the life he'd left behind, he supposed. Spare a thought for what they might be up to, far along the road he'd left untravelled. Yes — one day.

'Mary, then?' he asked. Gladys smiled, little fingers twined tightly round her own.

'Mary,' she said. And that was that.

1st January, 1922

'There are many possible futures, do you see? All laid out like, like branching railway lines, I suppose. You're familiar with them, I would imagine?'

They were back in the station, variously huddled by the grate, or pacing between the door and the filing nook while Mr. Dogberry attempted to explain the situation to an uncomprehending, increasingly erratic Frank. 'He's not dead, he's just missing!' he screamed back. Dogberry didn't seem to notice. Or perhaps he was just hoping the explanations would end up in Frank's ears at some point, which by now seemed to be the only way to operate.

'Can't tell if I did or didn't,' added Sergeant Whitney from the desk, still scribbling intently in his notebook, 'I've been lost since you started.'

Clarissa knew the feeling. But the words didn't ring any bells in the part of her mind that had begun, inevitably, to try to process this new form of communication. File it away in the drawer of spare jigsaw pieces of conversation, wait for someone to ask him the question, put it in context...

It was quite dark outside by now, the windows turned to a dim looking-glass by the gaslight. How long would that keep working, Clarissa wondered. How long before they froze, thirsted, starved to death?

'But only one future actually happens, naturally. At any given moment the points, if you will, are set according to people's actions, and so the engine of the present rattles off down that particular line.'

Sergeant Whitney looked up, with the frown of someone hearing the conversation in the wrong direction. 'Now, hang about. You mean to say something our Constable did back in the past has led to all this butchery? Ending all life on Earth?'

Dogberry gave a dark little chuckle. 'Good lord, no. How on earth would he manage that? Look, I'll tell you what, could you draw us a railway line, Sergeant? With a set of points?'

Of course, Clarissa realised, that's what the poor man had been drawing all this time; that scrawled, sprawling mess of lines: a pair of tracks diverging. And a handful of words spilled from her box of jigsaw pieces: I don't know much about railways. She crossed that off her mental list of non-sequiteurs too. It was all oddly satisfying, just like a jigsaw puzzle in fact, although, she was well aware, just like a jigsaw puzzle, entirely futile. They would still starve.

In fact the only thing that kept her from walking out into the darkness right now was the vain hope that somebody might say 'That's right, all we have to do is push this hidden lever in the casement, and we'll be whisked back to 1887 in a trice!'

'That's right, she...she's at the grocer's,' Frank sobbed. Clarissa bit back a hollow laugh. So close. And cast her mind back: yes, why hasn't your mother or father come to the station, no answer. Another one down. It did feel like solving a crossword somehow, like she was crossing out the options. And when they were out of options...

'Now, you see, life comes along the track, chuffta-chuff, and then – you see?' Mr. Dogberry was holding the diagram in front of Frank's face, pointing at it with his pencil. 'Once it goes down a particular route, all those other potential futures, the ones that didn't happen, are left dead and empty. But by leaving Constable Wilson in the past, we've switched the points on the railway track of history: redirected the engine of, of reality, if you like, to rattle along in a different world, one that has him living in it. Nobody actually dies, heavens no. Life goes on, just as it should... except that it's jolted down that track instead. All those souls, all those missing lives – your grandfather – carrying on in another world altogether.'

He paused. He looked so lonely, somehow. 'Which leaves this one, our world, time as it should be, as one of those dead futures. An untravelled path. Just an empty, lifeless husk of what might have been. Life never reached it, you see – except for us. And that means there's no way out. We have nothing left to pull us back on course.'

The gaslight flickered out.

Clarissa's heart lurched. And suddenly, without warning, Mr. Dogberry swung around, staring right at her, eyes wide in the darkness. 'Well if we can find a way to do that, this whole ghastly future will never have happened, and the police station will return to functionality!'

She froze. This was it. The answer! She hardly dared breathe, in case she broke the slender thread of cause and effect that linked them. 'Do what, Mr. Dogberry? Isiah? Do what? That's the key to everything, it means we can escape back into 1887, rescue Constable Wilson!'

He said nothing. And, inevitably, she rolled back their words, looked for the gaps, the cul-de-sacs, the jigsaw-puzzle holes to fill... and realised there were none.

They had both been replying to each other.

It was starting to get cold.

18th October 1910

'Mister Wilson?'

Wilson stared at the boy. Or the man, he supposed he should say. Fresh-faced little bachelor, polished cheeks, hair clicked down specially. And a moustache that made him look even younger. What was he, twenty? Twenty-one? Not even half Wilson's age. But then, the same age, as the crow flies.

He coughed. 'You've, er... You've discussed this with Mary, have you?'

'I an't asked her, if that's what you mean, Mister Wilson sir. Wouldn't be proper.'

The voice was heavy with broad Cheshire vowels, rolling as the hills. Like Mary's own. 'Only you have to understand, she is still very young...'

'She's 19, Mister Wilson sir. Sorry, sir.'

Grief. Where had all the years gone? He'd stopped looking for the others, he realised. Still hadn't told Gladys the truth. Hometown? Parents? Job? Somehow it had all just stopped mattering, eventually.

There were other things to think about.

'It's just, sir... that we are in love, you see. We are very much in love.'

Wilson leant back in his seat, his back griping as he shifted, and gave the boy a long, hard stare. Could be worse. 'Well, you just listen to me, George. It is George, isn't it? You look after her. Look after both of you. 'Cos the next few years – the next few years...

'You just look after her.'

1st January, 1922

A hand passed her a plate in the darkness. She handed it on round to the left without taking anything; it wouldn't do to seem greedy, not now. Besides, Frank needed them more than Clarissa did, even if he didn't know it, skinny little thing. Once these buns were gone, these paltry last few morsels, then they really were done for.

The four of them were seated in a circle, wearing their coats buttoned up to the necks: faint shadows in the dark. The fire had long since gone out, with no wood outside to replenish it. Of course they could always burn the furniture, but somehow that felt like giving in. And they had given in, really they had, only... she couldn't put her finger on it. A nagging feeling, like when you've left a clue hanging in a story and forgotten to have the detective account for it.

'For instance,' said Mr. Dogberry out of nowhere, 'We may both have experienced this conversation in a different order, and Sergeant Whitney over there in another one altogether.'

Clarissa barely looked up. The final jigsaw pieces falling into place, presumably: she was past caring how they fitted together.

'Still, I dare say we all make sense to ourselves. Something of a moral there.'

He fell silent again. It was happening less and less often now, these sudden outbursts, as they huddled in the deepening silence. Over on the other side of the circle, Sergeant Whitney finally collapsed under the social pressure and ate the last of the buns.

There was something, though. Something that didn't fit. Some piece she hadn't quite noticed was in the wrong hole...

The plate came back round to her, bare of all but crumbs. No-one seemed to want to be the one to end the ritual of its passage, and admit they really were out of food. Or hope. Or—

She stopped. Stared.

Whitney had eaten the last of the buns. But she'd sent Wilson out to get buns, because they had run out.

'Oh, good lord...' she whispered. All this time they'd been trying to work out what had gone wrong with the station, what had caused these terrible problems, and yet... 'Don't you see, time is running out for us, because of something further along a track it wasn't on at the time when it was going to have happened!'

They stared at her. 'What?' asked Sergeant Whitney at last, which was about as much use as he'd been all day.

Alright, it wasn't her finest hour for eloquence, she had to admit. Or lucidity. Or not panicking. Or not being on the very, very edge of dying of cold and starvation with a head-ache that was really beginning to—

No, no, calm, careful. She stilled herself, closed her eyes, breathed in. 'Clearly, since causality has dissolved, it makes sense that some effects of our predicament predate the problem itself,' she said. 'So, I hypothesise, there is a very good reason why we haven't been able to deduce what's gone wrong with the station.'

'Oh, shut up about your stupid calendar! I barely touched it.'

And she stared at him. Funny how you miss what's right in front of you. 'It hasn't happened yet.'

7th August, 1911

Mary beamed at them shyly, her hand in George's. Wilson remembered that feeling: the first time you told. Should have seen it himself, he thought; pinafore like that, in this weather. He was getting old.

'No, but that's wonderful,' he said, 'Wonderful! I'm delighted for you.'

He glanced at Gladys. Camped out in the shade behind the house, sheet drawn up over the chair to shield her from the worst of the insects, she almost looked well. 'We both are,' he added, and her face crinkled into a smile, squeezing his hand. He'd forgotten how warm, how wonderful this summer was going to be, despite everything.

'Mary was saying, weren't you Mary? That we wanted to name him – or her, or, you know, whichever they are – after one of you. If that's alright.'

'You hear that, ma?' Mary prompted, just a little too loud. 'Another Gladys!'

Oh, as if there ever could be. But she perked up at that, the way she always used to, the old make-believe scowl on her face. 'Funny name for a boy, Constable,' she tutted.

And they laughed, for as long and as loud as they could. While summer lasted.

1st January, 1922

Frank staggered back from the hearth, wide eyes brimming as Clarissa advanced on him. 'You're an idiot, Frank Draycott!' she screamed. And to think, she'd wondered why he'd looked so scared of her. 'Oh, no wonder you're sobbing. No wonder you're such a snivelling little crybaby. You're scared, aren't you? Scared of the truth!'

'I say, steady on,' muttered the sergeant, as if dragged into the present by the sheer force of her vitriol. Even Mr. Dogberry looked perturbed. But there was no choice: what's done is, or at any rate had to be, done.

'Coming in here, telling us your grandfather is missing. Missing! We should charge you with wasting police time! Of course he isn't missing. You said yourself, your mother's at the grocer's. But it isn't a grocer's any more, is it? We just keep calling it that because we don't like to say what it's become. Finn's is the *undertakers*, Frank.'

He shook his head, eyes red with tears. His broken sobs were the only other sound in the station. But what else could she do, when the consequences were all around them? She knew what it was to lose someone, to miss them – to live in denial of it, even. But she had to open his eyes.

'We all know what happened last night. Look at it, right there on the calendar: New Year's Eve. You'll never be able to forget it, will you? You'll always hear those bells, that dreadful song... and you'll remember him, dying.'

His face was clenched into a red rage now, wet with snot and tears and anger. 'Shut up, shut up, shut up...'

'Because, do you know something, Frank? He is missing. Now and always. That's all death is: a puzzle you can never solve. Someone will be first across your threshold, on those bitter winter mornings, to bring you the new year... But I'm sorry, Frank. I truly am. But it will never be him.'

It was like a shotgun going off, when it finally happened. All that pent-up anger, all that accumulated fear and rage let out in one long, young scream, as he tore the calendar from the wall, piece by piece. Great fistfuls of days at a time, ripped away from the cardboard backing, hurled into the air and drifting down like a great blizzard, all around them.

All those random times mixed up into a strange new order, without rhyme or reason, cut entirely adrift from causality.

He threw the rest of it at her head, in the end. And in the privacy of her own skull, a little part of Clarissa Miller ticked off the jigsaw piece marked 'head-ache', and went for a lie down.

28th September, 1918

The sound was excruciating. It crept in through the plaster walls, muffled, but filling the room completely.

Wilson stood in the middle of it, stranded and helpless. Everything felt so stupid. The world had turned grey in a moment, all the scenery of his life revealed as empty flats. He couldn't believe the nerve of the daisies, still bright amid the sobs, daring to shine in their pot beside the crumpled message.

REGRET TO INFORM, it exhorted, implausibly. CPL GEORGE DRAYCOTT, it persisted. PRESUMED, it whispered, furtive, insistent.

He'd tried so hard. Kept him back from volunteering. Steered him from the Somme. And for what? Two months short. Two bloody months.

'Come here, lad,' he said, eventually. How long had they been there, those big, wide eyes, staring at him from the hallway? Too young to pretend not to hear.

'Is he...dead?' the boy asked, in a tiny voice. 'Like Nanny Wilson?'

At least it was raining. Anything else would have been unbearable.

'Don't say that, Frank. Never say that. You'll break your ma's heart. Da's...well, he's missing, that's what it says, isn't it? He's just...missing.'

1st January

All was silent.

Outside the window, a blank, white void.

The rug was scattered with torn and shredded days, the empty nail on the wall jutting out at them accusingly.

'Ah, now, not to worry about that, Miss,' said Sergeant Whitney, and it took Clarissa a moment to realise he was actually addressing her, and the situation, in the here and now. 'As it happens I have something put aside for this very sort of eventuality. You never know when a spare bit of stationery's going to prove useful, do you?'

He crossed to the desk and rummaged about for a moment in the bottom drawer of things that were bound to come in handy some day, before triumphantly producing a new day-calendar, fresh and untouched. He popped it on the nail, beaming.

'There we are, you see! It's the wrong year, mind, I'll give you that. But when's that ever stopped us, eh?'

The sergeant gave a hearty, wheezing laugh. And with a sudden jangle of the bell above the door, Constable Wilson burst in, fresh-faced from the cold, with his arms piled with bulging paper bags, and the sounds of the street hot on his heels, clattering and shouting and hammering home that they were here, where they had started, in 1887.

Clarissa shook her head. Of course 1887. When else would it be?

'Buns!' cried Wilson, scattering the desk with his newfound riches. For some reason it felt like an absolute age since he'd left. 'Tea! No Typhoo I'm afraid, apparently they haven't come up with it yet. But look – I may not be tall or dark, but you'll have to admit, we are all strangers 'round these parts.'

Yes, he had a lump of coal with him. Because of course, he was the first to cross the threshold today. Naturally. 'How very droll,' Miss Miller said, not quite managing a smile. 'And – wasn't there...?'

Mr. Dogberry frowned. 'Yes, there was definitely something,' he murmered. 'Or... Something else we were supposed to find, maybe...'

'Really?' asked Sergeant Whitney. He seemed perfectly happy with his tea and buns and sundries. And now she came to think about it, Clarissa couldn't put her finger on what else she could possibly want.

It was irksome, though. Like a jigsaw puzzle, with just one piece missing.

'No, no, I checked,' said Wilson, assured as ever, tossing down her shopping list with his usual youthful swagger, every item ticked off in clumsy policeman's pencil. 'And I promise you, Miss Miller: this time there really is nothing missing at all.'

31st December, 1921

His lungs creaked with every breath. His bones ached. The gaslight danced in front of his waning eyes. Couldn't be long now.

'It's alright, you don't have to speak,' Mary murmured beside him. He could feel her hand on his, he thought. Frank too, maybe, in the shadows.

'I have...to tell you,' he gasped. God, the effort. And to think, he was out there now, young, strong-limbed, fighting crime, or at least dodging paperwork. If he could only reach the window to see.

'Shh, Da. It's alright.'

All these years, he'd never told them. Not George. Not his beloved Gladys. No-one. And they had a right, didn't they? His own family.

'I just...I need you to know, I'm...I'm really...'

He could hear distant bells ringing in the new year. Voices joining in the song, all around them. All of Manleigh Halt, together, in the cold.

Wilson smiled. Took one last breath. '...home.'